BUZZ AROUND THE TRACK

They Said It

"I'm good enough to drive in the NASCAR Sprint Cup Series—no doubt about it. My car doesn't care about gender, and Pebble Valley Wines shouldn't, either. I'm the right driver for the sponsorship, no doubt about it. All I have to do is prove it."
—Shelly Green

"Shelly is something else. The first time we met, she transformed right before my eyes. In the midst of our argument, she went from an awkward, ill-at-ease girl to a confident, self-assured spitfire of a woman— and a damn attractive one, at that."
—Damon Tieri

"Shelly deserves a car in the NASCAR Sprint Cup Series, but that doesn't mean she won't have to work hard to get it."
—Adam Sanford

"My daughter Mattie is a reporter. She won't stop looking into the Cargill murder, even though there is a new suspect. The story is important to her, but I can't let her investigation interfere with picking the right driver for Pebble Valley's future."
—Steve Clayton

KRISTINA COOK

Georgia native Kristina Cook practically grew up at the race track, watching her father race sports cars and working timing and scoring—once she was old enough to do the math, that is. Now married and living in New York City with her husband and two daughters, Kristina still loves racing and all things NASCAR. The author of more than half a dozen historical romances, Kristina is delighted to combine her enthusiasm for NASCAR with her love for writing romance. You can visit Kristina online at www.kristinacook.com.

NASCAR

FORCE OF NATURE

Kristina Cook

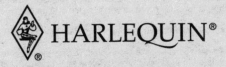

HARLEQUIN®

TORONTO • NEW YORK • LONDON
AMSTERDAM • PARIS • SYDNEY • HAMBURG
STOCKHOLM • ATHENS • TOKYO • MILAN • MADRID
PRAGUE • WARSAW • BUDAPEST • AUCKLAND

ISBN-13: 978-0-373-18529-0

FORCE OF NATURE

For my dad, Randy.
Finally, this one's for you!

NASCAR HIDDEN LEGACIES

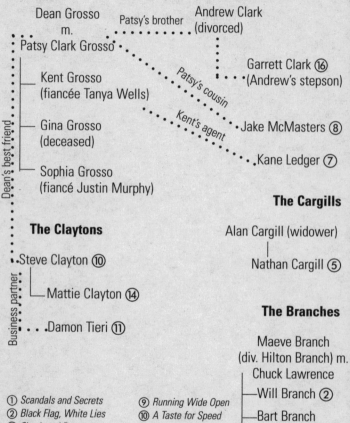

The Grossos

Dean Grosso
m.
Patsy Clark Grosso

— Kent Grosso
(fiancée Tanya Wells)

— Gina Grosso
(deceased)

— Sophia Grosso
(fiancé Justin Murphy)

Patsy's brother

The Clarks

Andrew Clark
(divorced)

Garrett Clark ⑯
(Andrew's stepson)

Patsy's cousin

Jake McMasters ⑧

Kent's agent

Kane Ledger ⑦

Dean's best friend

The Claytons

Steve Clayton ⑩

— Mattie Clayton ⑭

Damon Tieri ⑪

Business partner

The Cargills

Alan Cargill (widower)
|
Nathan Cargill ⑤

The Branches

Maeve Branch
(div. Hilton Branch) m.
Chuck Lawrence

— Will Branch ②

— Bart Branch

— Penny Branch m.
Craig Lockhart

— Sawyer Branch
(fiancée
Lucy Gunter)

THE FAMILIES AND THE CONNECTIONS

The Sanfords

Bobby Sanford
(deceased)
m.
Kath Sanford

— Adam Sanford ①

— Brent Sanford ⑫

— Trey Sanford ⑨

The Hunts

Dan Hunt
m.
Linda (Willard) Hunt
(deceased)

— Ethan Hunt ⑥

— Jared Hunt ⑮

— Hope Hunt ⑫

— Grace Hunt Winters ⑯
(widow of Todd Winters)

The Mathesons

Brady Matheson
(widower)
(fiancée Julie-Anne Blake)

— Chad Matheson ③

— Zack Matheson ⑬

— Trent Matheson
(fiancée Kelly Greenwood)

The Daltons

Buddy Dalton
m.
Shirley Dalton

— Mallory Dalton ④

— Tara Dalton ①

— Emma-Lee Dalton

CHAPTER ONE

June, Loudon, New Hampshire

"HOW'S IT FEEL, SHELLY?"

Shelly eased off the throttle and went low in Turn Three, taking the bottom groove. "It's way too loose—keeps getting out from under me. I'm going to end up in the wall."

"Ten-four, chickadee. Bring it on in next time around, and we'll make some quick adjustments."

"Will do." Shelly sped through Turn Four, her pulse racing through her veins like quicksilver. Damn, but this car was fast. If they could just tighten it up a bit, they might be able to get themselves a much-needed win.

"Whoa," Al's voice came through on her headset as she roared past the start/finish line. "Loose or not, you're the fastest car on the track right now. That lap was twenty-nine-point-nine-four-four. Yee-haw!"

Grinning, Shelly pressed the mike button. "Maybe some wedge and a tiny bit of air pressure, Al. That should do it."

"A quarter-pound?"

"Maybe just a tenth. Here I come, boys." Reaching the commitment cone, Shelly laid off the throttle and ducked down onto pit road.

"Watch your speed, Shel. That's it. Just a splash of fuel and two tires, okay?"

"Got it." Keeping an eye on the tachometer, she cruised to her pit stall, pulling in sharply as she hit the brakes.

No more cautions, she silently prayed as she took a quick drink of tepid water. There was no way they could make it on fuel to the end—not even close—but neither could anyone else. Still, they'd been the first of the lead-lap cars to pit under green, always a risk. But the risk out there was greater, running as loose as they were. Especially with Kyle Jordan on her tail, breathing down her neck.

Fourteen-point-two seconds later, she peeled out of her box—just ahead of Jordan, who had followed her in. "Great stop, boys," she said.

"Just stay out in that clean air, Shelly," came Al's voice. "Twenty to go once you cross the line."

From that point on, Shelly concentrated on hitting her marks, checking the rearview mirror every now and then, watching Kyle Jordan fall farther and farther back.

"Looks like Castillo is going to take Jordan," came her spotter's voice a few laps later.

Adrenaline surged through Shelly's veins as she rounded Turn Two, moving into some lapped traffic. "Aw, Rick, don't you worry. Castillo's got nothing for us today."

"Who said I was worried?" came Rick's reply. "Clear high. Clear all around."

"Five to go, Shelly. The little chickadee is flying now, ain't she?"

"Can it, Al," she chastised, though she couldn't help but smile. Truthfully, the chickadee thing was starting to grow on her, though she'd never let Al know. He only did it to irritate her—he thought she drove better when she was irritated.

Maybe she did. Didn't matter, not right now. All that mattered was that she continued to hit her marks, and that the field stayed green for four more laps. Four more just like this one and she'd have her second win of the year, just one less than Kyle Jordan, the current NASCAR Nationwide Series points leader.

Despite Shelly's win back at 'Dega, she was currently fourth in points, thanks to a run of bad luck that had started with a bad finish at Dover. They needed this win, and badly. Word had it that Steve Clayton's Pebble Valley Winery was looking to sponsor a NASCAR Sprint Cup Series car next year, and they were taking a look at some of the most promising NASCAR Nationwide Series drivers. Shelly wanted that sponsorship.

"Next time by, you'll take the white flag," came Al's voice in her headset. She could hear his excitement, though he tried to hide it. Truth was, after two years of working together, she could read Al Spencer like a book. Probably why they made such a great team.

"Here comes the checkered flag!" Al all but hollered, making Shelly wince even as she grinned. "You got it! Yahoo!"

"Great job, Shelly," came Rick's voice, full of pride.

Shelly waved one fist in the air as she crossed the start/finish line, Roberto Castillo nearly half a lap behind in second position. "Thanks, guys! Everyone did a great job today. You're the best."

Not bad for a small-town girl from Alabama, she thought, smiling in self-satisfaction. She'd come a long way from that little dirt track in the northeast corner of the state where the soil was a deep, brick red and kudzu ran rampant.

She'd all but grown up there at the track. Missy Green had been a single mom struggling to make ends meet. She'd worked two jobs to put food on their table—checking at the local Grocery Barn during the day, and running the concessions at the track at night. There was never enough money for a babysitter, so while Missy worked, Shelly sat up in the grandstand bleachers for hours on end, completely enthralled by the slip-sliding action on the other side of the chain-link fence.

She'd been racing karts by the time she was ten, mucking out stalls at a nearby stable to earn money since more often than not any extra cash Missy had went straight to the local liquor store.

And while other girls her age were hanging out at the mall and going on dates, she was busy clawing her way up the ranks, racing everything from midgets to late-models to modifieds—and winning every title imaginable. She'd gotten her big break when Adam Sanford had come to their little dirt track to watch her in action. He'd offered her a ride in Sanford Racing's NASCAR

Nationwide Series car on the spot. She'd left Alabama right then and there, and never looked back.

And now she was climbing out of the No. 411 Zippi-Print car in Victory Lane to a shower of champagne, her team surrounding her in a big group hug as they whooped it up. Today's win had moved her into second place in points. Sure, it was still early in the season, but she'd proven that she could hang with the big boys.

She was good enough to drive in the NASCAR Sprint Cup Series—there was no doubt about it. Even Adam thought she could do it. Only problem was, fielding a second NASCAR Sprint Cup car was expensive. Sanford Racing would have to snag a huge sponsorship deal even to consider it, which is where Pebble Valley Wines came in. All she had to do was convince Steve Clayton and his investors that she was the right man— well, the right *woman* in this case—for the job.

Shelly reached up to adjust her purple hat, pulling her ponytail through the opening in the back just as the Victory Lane reporter shoved a microphone in her face.

"Congratulations on your first win at Loudon, Shelly. How's it feel?"

"It feels good," she answered with a smile, a plan forming in her mind even as she spoke.

Time to be proactive. She'd fly to Steve's winery in the Sonoma Valley herself—first thing Monday morning—and plead her case.

"As the only female driver in the NASCAR Nationwide Series, do you feel any added pressure to prove yourself?" the reporter asked.

She got this question all the time. It was getting kind of old, actually, but she just smiled for the cameras as she gave the same answer she always did. "Nah, not really. I've got the best team possible, and I think my skills speak for themselves," she said confidently. "Besides, the car doesn't really care what chromosomes the driver's got."

And it shouldn't matter to Steve Clayton and Pebble Valley Wines, either, she mentally added. She was the right one for the sponsorship, no doubt about it.

All she had to do was prove it.

DAMON TIERI REACHED for the remote, muting the volume on the enormous flat-screen television that dominated the wall opposite where he sat. "That's Shelly Green's second win of the season, isn't it?" he asked, watching the woman in question toss her blond ponytail over one shoulder as she soundlessly answered the reporter's questions.

It was hard to believe she was old enough to drive, much less drive a race car in the NASCAR Nationwide Series. She looked more like someone's kid sister, he thought, watching as the camera panned in on her face, the close-up revealing a sprinkling of freckles across the bridge of her nose.

Someone's *cute* kid sister, he amended.

"She's good," Steve Clayton said, then took a swig of beer.

Damon just nodded, reaching for his own beer. "Kyle Jordan looked strong. I wonder what happened there at the end?"

Steve just shrugged. "He didn't have anything for No. 411 car. Green was fast all weekend. I told you, she's good."

"You're sure a NASCAR sponsorship is the way to go?" Damon asked, the same old doubts creeping back into his mind. He couldn't help it—he was a money man, and sponsoring a NASCAR team was damn expensive.

"It's the best publicity we can get, and it makes sense to use my connections to NASCAR," Steve said. After all, he'd been a NASCAR champion before he'd retired to become a vineyard owner and apprentice winemaker, under the tutelage of Kyle Markham. "But we need to sponsor someone young. An upstart, someone smart and successful."

Damon nodded. "Someone like Kyle Jordan, you mean."

"Not necessarily. Besides, I don't want to rush into any decision. You need to get to know the sport a little better first, and then we'll talk about narrowing down the candidates."

Steve had a point. Damon was new to NASCAR, new to racing in general. It was all a far cry from Wall Street, where he'd made a fortune not just for himself, but for his clients, too. Tieri Capital Management had been one of the industry's most profitable hedge funds, earning a near-record sum before the market had become unstable, at least to Damon's practiced eye. He'd gotten out just before the crash, earning his peers' awe and admiration and his clients' eternal gratitude.

Everyone—his father included—thought the time

was ripe to launch a new fund, but Damon just wanted to slow down, to focus on his future. What better way than to partner with Steve Clayton? After all, Damon enjoyed the finer things in life—expensive suits, fine cuisine, excellent wines. And with champion wine-maker Kyle Markham and Steve Clayton, Pebble Valley Winery was positioned to be among the best in the world. They just weren't marketed well, and that was something Damon planned to rectify.

Besides, with the current situation on Wall Street, investing in a winery—especially one with Steve Clayton's name behind it—seemed like a far safer hedge. With his business acumen, Steve's image and Kyle Markham's natural talent for winemaking, they were sure to be a success.

All they needed was the right driver to serve as the 'face' of Pebble Valley. Someone good-looking and well-spoken enough for a national ad campaign. Steve was right, Damon realized. This wasn't a decision they should rush into. He glanced back at the television screen, at Shelly Green, who was now hoisting a trophy in the air with a triumphant smile. It was infectious, the way it lit up her face, and he couldn't help but smile back at the TV as he hit Stop on the DVD player.

"So Kent Grosso is out, then?" Damon said as he laid down the remote.

Steve nodded. "I'm afraid so. Actually, I really want to find a diamond in the rough, someone we can help make a star. Let's just focus on the NASCAR Nation-wide drivers."

"Makes sense. What time is your flight to Daytona?" Damon asked, glancing down at his stainless-steel watch.

"Brent Sanford is meeting me at the airstrip at three," Steve said, checking his own watch. "I should probably get going."

"I'll probably stay a couple of more days," Damon said. "I've still got a lot to catch up on here, but I'll head down to Daytona by the end of the week."

"Sounds good. Make yourself at home, and let Rosita know if you need anything."

Damon nodded. "I appreciate it." His cell phone began to vibrate against his hip. He reached for it, glancing at the number displayed. Courtney. He'd call her back later.

"Just give me a call if you have any questions. And it probably wouldn't hurt to watch the rest of the DVDs there." Steve tipped his head toward the stack of cases piled up beside the DVD player. "I've got all the NASCAR Nationwide races back to Daytona in February. See if anyone stands out to you."

"Sure will," Damon agreed, reaching for Steve's hand and giving it a friendly shake. "Have a safe trip back."

A HALF HOUR LATER, Damon stood thumbing through the stack of DVDs, a glass of Pebble Valley's excellent Merlot in one hand. It was only then that he remembered that Courtney had called. He dug out his cell, looking to see if she'd left a message.

She hadn't, and he was surprised by the sense of

relief he felt. He'd been dating Courtney Snow off and on for four years now, and things had grown stale. It wasn't that he didn't care about her—he did care, quite a bit. Their relationship was easy, comfortable, predictable, even. But something was missing, something he couldn't quite put his finger on.

His family adored her, of course. She was exactly the type of woman they expected him to marry—beautiful, well-educated, from a good family. On paper, she was perfect. Only his heart wasn't entirely convinced, and time was running out. They'd reached a stalemate of sorts. He either needed to propose or permanently end it—he wasn't sure which.

Ending it would probably break his mother's heart more than Courtney's, if truth be told, and maybe that was answer enough. Still, he'd spent a lifetime doing exactly what his family expected of him, and it was a hard habit to break. But marriage? He needed to be a hundred-percent sure before he made a commitment like that.

Whatever the case, he really wasn't interested in talking to Courtney right now. Instead, he took the case marked Daytona—February and opened it up, taking out the disc and popping it into the slot on the front of the machine.

The darkened screen flickered to life, and Damon headed toward the leather chair he'd occupied earlier, taking his wineglass with him.

Just as he sat down, the doorbell chimed. "Rosita?" he called out.

He waited, listening for the housekeeper's quick footsteps, but the house remained silent. The bell chimed again.

Puzzled, Damon hit the stop button on the remote and strode off toward the front hall, setting his wineglass down on the hall console.

"Can I help you?" he asked as he pulled open the door to find a woman standing there, her back to him.

Looking as if he'd startled her, the woman turned to face him, peering up at him curiously with big, crystal-clear blue eyes. Shelly Green, he realized at once. The same woman he'd just seen hoisting the trophy on TV.

"I'm here to see Steve Clayton," she said, her voice a smooth, Southern drawl. She looked every bit the sweet little-sister type she'd looked on TV, with her flowery sundress and blond ponytail.

"I, uh…I'm afraid you just missed him. I'm Damon Tieri. Steve's business partner," he added. He offered his hand, but she didn't seem to notice, so he let it drop back to his side. "It's pretty hot out there—why don't you come on in?"

Her eyes narrowed a fraction, and then she glanced back over her shoulder, toward the car in the gravel drive. As if she were measuring the distance, preparing to flee.

"I promise you I'm not dangerous," he said with a smile. "Unless you get me near the kitchen, that is. Besides, I'm pretty sure there's a housekeeper around here somewhere. But make up your mind, because you're letting all that hot air—" he gestured toward the open doorway "—in here."

"Who did you say you were again?" she asked as she brushed past him into the foyer.

"Damon Tieri," he answered. "And you're Shelly Green."

"Well," she drawled, "now that that's out of the way…"

CHAPTER TWO

SHELLY BLINKED HARD, trying to adjust her eyes as she stepped out of the bright California sun and into the dim foyer. She took a deep, calming breath, hoping it would bolster her confidence. Truth was, now that she was there, she felt anything *but* confident, despite her carefully laid-out plan.

"They told me that Steve would be here today," she said, glancing around, feeling oddly underdressed in her best clothes compared to the man who stood before her looking completely comfortable in a white button-down shirt and jeans. An expensive pair of jeans, she mentally added. They fit him *way* too well to be anything but.

"Yeah, we finished up our business earlier than we expected, and he took an afternoon flight out. Sorry about that."

Shelly just nodded, swallowing hard. This Damon Tieri made her a little tongue-tied. He was too good-looking, like a movie star or something. Dark hair, dark eyes and a killer smile that would make any woman's knees go weak. As he stood watching her, he raked a hand through his wavy hair, lending a slight air of dishevelment to his otherwise perfect appearance.

He was over six feet tall, Shelly guessed—a good half-foot taller than her five foot six—and powerful looking. Not necessarily overly muscled like a jock, but strong and fit. Actually, he kind of reminded her of a sleek, shiny thoroughbred. She forced herself to avert her gaze before he noticed her checking him out.

"I...uh, can I get you something?" he asked her. "Some water? Or a glass of wine?"

She cleared her throat uncomfortably. "Some water would be great."

"Sure. Here, why don't you sit down." He led her into a living room and gestured toward a big leather couch. Shelly followed him as if in a daze, nodding like an idiot as she sat where he'd indicated.

"Do you prefer still or mineral?"

"What?" she asked, confused.

"Water," he clarified, rubbing his jaw with the palm of one hand. A very chiseled jaw, she noticed, with just the right amount of stubble. Maybe he had been a model in the past, because normal people just didn't look like that—at least, not where she came from. "Still or mineral?" he prodded.

Shelly still wasn't sure what he was asking her. "Just plain water is fine," she said with a shrug. "You know, the stuff that comes from the tap?"

He narrowed his eyes, then nodded, hooking a thumb toward the hallway they'd just come from. "I'll just be a second."

What do I do now? she wondered, unable to believe she'd come all this way for nothing. *Stupid, stupid.* She drummed her fingers against the arm of the couch, suddenly wishing she had just turned around and left rather than accepting Mr. Hollywood's offer of water.

"Here you go," he said, striding back toward her with a bottled water in his outstretched hand. "I can get you a glass, if you'd like."

"No, this is fine. Thanks," she added, taking the cold bottle and pressing it against her neck. It felt good. She was hot and sticky from her ride up from the airport.

"So, it's good to meet you," he said, sprawling into the chair across from where she sat. "I was actually just watching Saturday's race. Steve taped it for me. That was some win."

"Yeah, thanks. Wait, why were you watching it?" she blurted out, unable to curb her curiosity.

His dark eyes met hers—deep, deep brown. So dark they looked almost black. "I've invested in Pebble Valley Winery. Full partnership. Steve and I are looking for a driver to sponsor, someone to be the face of Pebble Valley, and I'm just trying to get caught up—"

"That's exactly why I'm here," Shelly interrupted, scooting forward on the couch, wincing when her sweaty thighs made a sucking sound against the leather. "About the sponsorship."

"Really?" he asked, looking amused. "Now that's interesting."

Shelly prickled at once. "What's that supposed to mean?"

"Just that I'm surprised, that's all." He shrugged carelessly.

"Because I'm a girl?"

"I didn't say that," he shot back, folding his arms across his chest.

"Yeah, and I'm sure it never crossed your mind."

"Don't presume to know what I think, Miss Green. It *is* Miss, isn't it?"

"What exactly is it you do?" she asked, ignoring his question. "I mean, how'd someone like you end up partners with Steve Clayton?" He was nothing like the laid-back Clayton, that was for sure.

"I manage a hedge fund in New York. Or at least I did. Tieri Capital Management."

"A hedge fund?" Shelly asked, shaking her head. "What is that, some sort of banking thing?"

He nodded. "A private investment fund. Short selling, high-yield ratings."

Shelly had no idea what he was talking about. "So in plain English, you're a Wall Street guy?"

"I guess you could say that. Semi-retired. You know, since I'm here now, instead of there." With a cocky grin, he patted the arms of the chair.

Shelly couldn't help but notice his nails—they were perfectly trimmed, buffed to a shine. Not a hint of motor oil staining them, no cracks and chips like her own nails had. Suddenly self-conscious, she resisted the urge to tuck her hands under her thighs.

"And let me guess," she asked, "Ivy League, right?"

His smile was almost smug. "Princeton. Though I

went to Stanford for business school—not too far from here. That's when I became interested in this whole winemaking business."

"Of course," she said. She had him all figured out now. "And I bet you live on Park Avenue. You know, 'Putting on the Ritz,' and all that."

"Fifth Avenue, actually. I don't know why it is that people who aren't from New York always assume that Park is the best address, when anyone from the City knows it's really Fifth. Anyway—" he waved one hand in dismissal "—anything else you'd like to know?"

"No, I think that just about sums it up," she said glumly. A guy like Tieri wouldn't understand racing, which meant he wouldn't understand *her*.

"It's your turn, then," he said. "Let's start with where you're from."

"Alabama. But I've been in North Carolina for a couple of years now. In Mooresville."

"And what did you do back in Alabama?"

"Mostly hung out at the dirt track. My mom worked there on weekends, and that's where I got my start."

"Racing, you mean?"

"No, tap dancing," she answered, rolling her eyes.

A muscle in his jaw flexed, but he didn't respond to her jibe. "And what about your family?" he asked instead.

Shelly felt her cheeks burn. "My mom raised me alone. I, uh…I never met my father. But he was a driver—modifieds, I think. So I guess it's in my blood," she finished lamely. What did her family matter to him, anyway?

"And you went to school, I presume?"

"Sure, high school. There wasn't much point in college," she said defensively. "I was already racing, winning titles by the time I graduated."

"And what do you like to do when you're not racing?"

What was this, the Inquisition? "I don't know. I'm pretty much racing all the time."

He drummed his fingers against the arms of the chair. "You must have some free time. What do you do on off days?"

"Mostly hang around the shop," Shelly answered. "I'm a pretty skilled mechanic. I can build a motor from the ground up. But other than that, well…" She swallowed hard, racking her brain. "I like to ride. Horses, I mean. And I watch a lot of movies. Action, drama…" she trailed off with a shrug.

He nodded, then leaned back in his chair, folding his arms across his chest. "Well, let me tell you what kind of driver we're looking for. First and foremost, someone who shares some of the characteristics of the wine itself—sophisticated but fresh, an upstart in an established market. Someone articulate, cultured." His gaze was direct, unflinching. "It probably goes without saying that they should have a healthy appreciation for fine wine."

Shelly felt the heat rise in her cheeks. "That's some list," she said, trying to keep the edge of anger out of her voice. Why didn't he just come out and say 'someone who is absolutely, positively nothing like you'?

Damon nodded. "We're pretty particular. Let me cut to the chase, Ms. Green. I'm sure you're a perfectly capable driver, but I just don't think you're a good fit for Pebble Valley and our wines."

"You can call me Shelly," she said, her voice deceptively calm.

"Shelly, then. I'm sorry you came all the way out here for nothing."

She stood up, smoothing down her dress with shaking hands. "That's it, then? You interrogate me for five minutes, and already you know that I'm not right for the sponsorship?"

He rose, towering over her. "I think it's pretty obvious that—"

"That what?" she interrupted. "That I'm not good enough? I'm one of the best drivers in the series—you ask anyone involved with NASCAR and they'll tell you so. We had a little bit of bad luck there, but we got ourselves back on track this weekend."

"With two wins already, I'd say you're having a pretty good season so far," he said with a smile.

"But that's not good enough for you, is it? No, you stand there in your expensive clothes, with your expensive watch and Ivy League attitude, pretending like you know something about NASCAR, when it's obvious you haven't got a clue." She took a deep breath, her hands in fists by her sides.

"Let me tell you something about racing," she continued. "It takes a heck of a lot more than talent to make it in this sport. It takes years of sacrifice, of dedication.

I worked like a dog to get where I am today. And, being a girl, I had to work twice as hard as everyone else.

"They don't just hand you a NASCAR career on a silver platter, you know. You have to earn it. Everyone on your team's got to believe in you, trust in you one hundred percent. Racing isn't about being sophisticated or cultured or…or articulate," she sputtered. "It's about winning. About respect. About skill. And that's what *I'm* all about, Mr. Tieri. I'm the best there is. And if you're not smart enough to realize that, then maybe you should go back to Wall Street where you belong."

DAMON JUST STARED AT her, stunned, trying to make sense of Shelly's transformation right before his eyes. She'd somehow gone from an awkward, ill-at-ease girl who didn't look like she could promote a sack of beans to a confident, self-assured spitfire of a woman—and a damn attractive one, at that—in a matter of seconds.

"Wow," he said, shaking his head in amazement. "That was…something else."

"Oh, I'm just getting started," she answered, her eyes flashing angrily.

Damon held up one hand. "Wait. Just let me—"

"No, *you* wait." She pointed a finger at his chest. "You fuddy-duddy banker types with your old money and family connections have had your day. The future is for people with vision and determination and passion, no matter their background. And if that doesn't fit with Pebble Valley Winery, then you tell me what does."

Inwardly, he winced as her words hit their mark.

Somehow she'd managed to make him feel like a total ass, and it wasn't a feeling he enjoyed. There she stood, looking so eager, so earnest in her little flowered dress, and he'd never even given her a chance. Instead, he'd taken one look at her and made a snap judgment.

Yet snap judgments had never been his style. He'd always been one to think things through, to examine them from all angles before making a decision of any kind. On the other hand, his initial instincts usually proved to be right. And his initial instinct was telling him that she wasn't a good fit. But that didn't mean that he shouldn't at least give her the courtesy of considering it.

"You're right," he said at last, stroking his jaw ruefully. "And I owe you an apology."

Her eyes widened a fraction, as if he'd taken her by surprise. "Apology accepted."

"You've made some good points," he continued. "I'll talk to Steve Clayton about it. About you," he corrected.

"I'd appreciate that," she said, her eyes meeting his, holding them. She seemed so young, so tiny, her head barely reaching his shoulder, and yet there was an air of authority, of strength about her.

More than anything, he was surprised by the jolt of physical attraction he felt—stronger than he'd felt for anyone in a long time. *Not good.* The last thing he needed was letting something like that cloud his judgment.

"Would you like to stay for dinner?" he said, before he'd thought better of it.

Mercifully, she shook her head. "No, I've got to get back. I flew commercial. Stand-by. I have no idea what I was thinking. Anyway, with Daytona coming up…" She trailed off with a shrug.

"Yeah, big race. I'll be there, actually. I'm flying down on Thursday."

"Well, I suppose I'll see you there, then." She reached for her bag and hoisted it onto one shoulder.

"Here, let me walk you to the car," he offered, leading her toward the front door. His arm brushed her shoulder, and one of her dress's thin straps slipped down.

"I think I can find it myself, thanks," she said, tugging the strap back to its rightful place, but not before Damon had an eyeful of the graceful slope between her neck and shoulder, the skin perfect and smooth and tanned.

I've been away from Courtney too long, he told himself, suddenly remembering that he'd never called her back. He would, later. After a shower—a very cold shower.

"So—" Shelly held out one hand "—it was good meeting you, Mr. Tieri."

Damon took it, surprised by the firmness of her handshake. "Definitely. And it's Damon. I'll…uh, see you in a few days."

"You sure will. And if I have my way, you'll see me win." She was confident again, her eyes sparkling with the challenge, her smile infectious and impossible to resist.

"Sounds good," he said with a grin, suddenly wishing she had taken him up on dinner. He opened the door and followed her out to the porch.

"Well, 'bye, then," she said with a wave, then hurried

to the white sedan in the drive, her sandals crunching the gravel beneath them.

Damon leaned back against the doorframe, watching as Shelly ducked into the car and sped away. He didn't move until the car was nothing but a speck of white in the distance against the bright-blue sky, and then he turned and walked back inside, shaking his head in amazement.

Steve was going to *love* this new development.

CHAPTER THREE

July, Daytona, Florida

SHELLY LAY HARD ON the throttle as she rolled out of Turn Four and headed for the straightaway, the start/finish line in sight. The letters spelling out *Daytona* blurred by as she roared across the line. A little loose, but it was hot out and the track was slick. It would be cooler come Friday night, so there would be more grip. Nothing to worry about.

"You just clocked the fastest practice speed," came Al's voice in Shelly's headset. "We must have done something right."

Shelly gripped the wheel tightly as she sailed through Turn One, grinning as she keyed the mike. "It feels like a rocket ship, Al. I don't remember the last time I had a car this good."

"That's what I like to hear. Why don't you bring it on in this time around?"

"Ten-four."

"Oh, and Shelly? Someone's here to see you."

"Oh, yeah?"

"Yeah, a suit. A nice suit, but a little fancy for the track."

Shelly laughed, shaking her head. "A suit came to see me, Al? Have you been sneaking something into your water bottle when no one's looking?"

"Don't give me any cheek." He was laughing now. "There's a man *in* the suit. Says he's here to see you. I told him he must've confused you with some other girl, but he ain't buying it."

"Oh, so now you're going to put on the good ol' boy act? Give it up, professor. Everyone knows you read Shakespeare. For *fun*," she added with a chuckle. Tugging the wheel to the left, she eased the car onto pit road, then made the turn toward the garage area.

Her heart did a little flip-flop as she considered her mystery guest in the suit. *Damon Tieri.* It was possible. After all, he'd said he was coming to Daytona. But wearing a suit, at the track, in the hot Florida sun?

Her pulse began to race, just like it did every time she thought about him. Which she'd done way too often since their little meeting on Monday, come to think of it.

Just a normal reaction, she assured herself as she pulled into her garage stall and cut the motor. After all, a lot was at stake. It had nothing to do with the fact that he was drop-dead gorgeous. No way—she was not *that* shallow.

Through her helmet's visor, she saw the man in question talking to the team's head engineer. Her breath hitched in her chest as recognition washed over her. It was Damon Tieri, all right. And he looked every bit as good as she remembered, too—same dark hair, same killer smile, same great ass.

Okay, maybe I am that shallow. She pulled off her driving gloves, forcing herself to take a few deep breaths, to get her hormones under control before she faced him. This was business, after all. And while she might be shallow, she certainly wasn't stupid. She wanted that sponsorship deal.

Taking her own sweet time, she unbuckled her seat restraints and removed her helmet and HANS device before dropping the net and climbing out the car's window.

"Hey, there, Tieri," she called out, forcing a careless tone into her voice. "Fancy meeting you here."

He turned toward her with a smile, and damn if her heart didn't do a little backflip. "Good to see you again," he said, extending a hand toward her.

So formal. She wiped her sweaty palm on her driving suit before shaking his hand. "That's some interesting trackside apparel you've got there. Ever considered a dress-down day?"

He laughed, the corners of his eyes crinkling. "Yeah, I had a business meeting this morning in New York. I haven't even had a chance to change yet," he explained a little sheepishly, and Shelly suddenly felt bad for teasing him. After all, she knew what it felt like to be a fish out of water. *Her life story.*

Don't screw this up, she told herself. *Talk about something neutral.* A bead of sweat ran down her neck. "Whew, it must be a million degrees today." She reached up to unzip her uniform.

For a second there, Damon's eyes widened. What did he think, that she was naked underneath? She

choked back a laugh as she pulled the zipper down—
his bewildered gaze following its path—and then tied
the sleeves around her waist. The skin-tight, fireproof
T-shirt she wore beneath her uniform clung wetly to her
skin, but there wasn't much she could do about it until
she got a shower.

"So," she said, then paused, waiting for him to raise
his gaze back to her face. "To what do I owe the pleasure?"

"Sorry," he said, shaking his head as if to clear it. "I
haven't talked to Steve yet, but I wanted you to know
that I'm thinking seriously about what you said. I'm here
to observe this weekend—you, in particular. Officially,
I'm a guest of Sanford Racing. I'll try not to get in your
way too much. Just try and think of me as your shadow."

Shelly exhaled slowly, trying to tamp down her excitement. Maybe she stood a chance, after all. Of course,
there was more to her excitement than that, as much as
she hated to admit it, even to herself. It sounded like she
was going to get to spend a lot of time with him this
weekend. *A lot.* And yeah, that made her pulse race
with anticipation.

"Wow," she said, forcing herself to focus. *Business.*
This was just business. He wasn't here to take her to the
prom. "Okay, so what next? I mean, how does this
whole thing work?"

He shrugged. "You just go about your normal routine. And I'll…just watch."

"Sounds kind of kinky," she said, smiling wickedly.
She couldn't help herself.

"Hey, did I hear the word *kinky?*" Al strode into the

garage, his headphones still around his neck. "Whatever it is, count me in."

Shelly rolled her eyes. "Damon, this is the best crew chief in NASCAR, Al Spencer. Al, Damon Tieri. Steve Clayton's new partner at the winery," she added meaningfully.

Al raised his eyebrows in understanding. "Ah, I see. Come to check out the little chickadee?"

"Enough with the chickadee thing, Al. You're really starting to annoy me."

"Well, it's a good thing I'm the best crew chief in NASCAR then, ain't it?" Al reached out a hand to Damon, and the two men shook. "Tieri, is it? Don't let 'er fool you. She might be a little thing, but she's a force of nature."

"I believe it," Damon said with a nod. "You should have heard her put me in my place the other day." He reached up to readjust his tie. "Not that I didn't deserve it."

Shelly just glared at the pair of them. "Are you done talking about me like I'm not standing right here?"

Damon nodded. "Actually, I'd like to spend a few minutes talking to Al, if it's okay with both of you."

"Sure," Al agreed. "I'd be happy to give you the low-down dirty on our girl here. Boy, do I have some stories to tell."

"Traitor!" Shelly said, folding her arms across her chest.

Al looked hurt. "Aw, c'mon now, Shel. You know me better'n that. They're all good stories."

"Whatever. I'll be in my motor home taking a shower. Make sure you knock if you decide to come by for a visit."

"I always do," Al retorted. "What do you take me for?"

"I meant him." She tipped her head toward Damon.

"Got it," Damon said. "Knock first."

"Have fun, boys." She blew a kiss to Al, then headed off toward the motor home lot.

DAMON WATCHED SHELLY saunter off, thinking just how well the phrase *force of nature* fit her. He'd watched the day's first practice from atop the team's hauler, utterly amazed that the little slip of a woman he'd seen on Monday was behind the wheel of that car, in total control of all that horsepower. Clearly, she was stronger than she appeared, more athlete than he'd imagined.

And even more clearly, her entire team—every single member he'd spoken to so far—adored her. Not only that, but they respected her. He might even go so far as to say they were all in complete awe of her.

"She's something else," Al said, shaking his head. "She acts all tough, but under that's a heart of gold."

"So I've heard," Damon muttered. "I'm just wondering what kind of spokesman…er, spokeswoman she'd make. That's an important part of our sponsorship agreement. We'd like to do a national ad campaign, both print and television spots."

Al nodded. "She's done some print ads for ZippiPrint. She's a pretty little thing," he said, sounding defensive.

"I mean, it's not like she cares much what she looks like when she's working, but she cleans up real nicely."

"I'm sure she does." The problem was, even 'cleaned up,' as Al put it, she still looked like someone's fresh-faced kid sister, which wasn't quite the sophisticated image they were going for. She barely looked past the legal drinking age, even though he knew for a fact that she was twenty-seven.

The question was, how much did that matter? He still thought Kyle Jordan was a better fit, but he couldn't stop thinking about Shelly. He needed to know more about her. Business research. Yeah, right.

"She's a good girl," Al offered. "Totally on the straight and narrow. I like to tease her, but she's like a daughter to me. I couldn't be prouder of her, both on the track and off. I have no doubt that she'll be a star one day soon. Heck, I just hope she takes me with her."

"She doesn't drink much, does she?" Damon asked. It was just a hunch, but he needed to know.

"Shelly? Naw, and for good reason," he added. "Maybe just a beer now and then."

That sounded pretty ominous. "What do you mean, for good reason?"

Al shrugged, turning back toward the car. "Well, I expect that's something Shelly can tell you herself."

Damon followed him, wondering if he could get him to say more, but someone wearing a green ZippiPrint polo shirt and carrying a clipboard intercepted him.

"Hey, Al, what's she need?"

"Not a thing. Says it's perfect. I think we'll stay with

racing trim for qualifying tomorrow. It's an impound race," Al directed at him, and Damon's attention shifted to the car.

It looked like a fine piece of machinery. An eye-catching sparkly green, with a purple ZippiPrint logo on the hood and a purple No. 411 outlined in black on the side.

"So that means no changes after qualifying?" he asked, running one hand along the fender.

"Yep, that's right. You been watching racing long?"

"Not really." Damon shook his head, then leaned into the open space where the window should be. "But I'm a quick learner. There's not much inside the cockpit. A lot of switches, though." It looked more like an airplane's controls than a car's dash.

"A lot of non-racing folks think it's pretty simple. You know, just press the pedal to the metal and keep turning left. But it's a lot more complicated than that."

"Yeah, I can see that." Damon pulled his head out of the car.

"She's ready for the NASCAR Sprint Cup Series," Al said. "Shelly, I mean. It's not always easy to find the right sponsor."

Damon just nodded.

Al eyed him suspiciously, and Damon realized it would take a while to earn this man's trust.

"It hasn't been an easy road for her. I hope you can appreciate that. It's more than luck that got her here. A hell of a lot more. Shelly's something special."

"That's the impression I'm getting from everyone

who knows her. I'm going to give her a chance, Al. As much a chance as anyone else. But in the end, I have to do what's right for us. For Pebble Valley. In today's economy, we just can't risk screwing up. I hope you can understand that."

In reply, Al held out one hand to him. Damon took it, shaking it firmly.

"Understood," Al said at last. "And I appreciate your honesty."

"Think she's done with her shower yet?" he asked.

"Long done. You know your way to the Drivers' and Owners' lot?"

Damon shook his head. "No idea."

Al swept one hand in front of him. "Then follow me."

A few minutes later, Al left him in front of a non-descript motor home, one that looked pretty much like the rest of them, except for the green trim. Stepping up to the door, he knocked loudly.

A dog barked—yipped was more like it—and then the door swung open. "No, Trixie, stay inside," Shelly said, reaching for a little white dog. "Sorry, just let me grab her and put her in the bedroom."

"She travels with you?" he asked when she returned. As he stepped up into the motor home, he ducked his head so he didn't whack it on the door frame.

"Of course. Most of the drivers travel with their pets. Wow, just how tall are you?"

"Six two," he said with a grin.

"Basketball?"

"No, lacrosse."

"Lacrosse?" She shook her head. "I'm pretty sure we didn't play that back in 'Bama."

"Well, imagine a combination of basketball, hockey and soccer, played on a field with long, webbed sticks. That pretty much covers it."

"Hmm. You learn something new every day."

"Now you know how I feel about NASCAR."

"Good," she said with a smile. "We're even, then. Come on in, make yourself comfortable." She led him toward a couch that faced a flat-screen TV hanging from the ceiling.

He took a seat, and she stood off to one side, leaning against what looked like a wet bar. Her hair was down— the first time he'd seen it out of its ponytail—and it was still damp, falling just past her shoulders in wheat-colored waves. His gaze traveled lower, past a black T-shirt that hugged her curves and khaki shorts, down the length of her legs to her bare feet. Her toenails were painted bright red—for some reason, that surprised him. Worse, it made his heart beat erratically. He suddenly felt like a hormonal teenager—not a good thing, given the current situation.

"Well," she said, eyeing him curiously. "What do you think of our sport so far?"

He dragged his gaze away from her feet, forcing himself into business mode. "It's fascinating. I love everything about it. The speed, the strategy." Now that his eyes had adjusted to the dim interior, he looked around, mostly trying not to look at her. "This is some motor home you've got here."

"Yeah, home sweet home. You should see some of

the NASCAR drivers' motor homes, though. They make this one look like a dump. Well, it *is* kind of a dump. I bought it used."

He could smell her scent—sweet, like coconut. Maybe it was her shampoo? Whatever it was, it was distracting the hell out of him.

She tilted her head to one side, watching him. "You look a little out of sorts. Can I get you something? A drink, maybe? I've got water, sweet tea, juice."

"No. Thanks. Sorry, I think the heat's getting to me. I usually try to avoid Florida in the summertime."

Her mouth twitched, as if she were suppressing a smile. "Well, you *could* take off your jacket, you know. I promise I won't tell anyone."

"Hmm, I guess I can trust you," he said with an easy laugh. "I wouldn't want to ruin my reputation as a total stiff, you know." He shrugged out of the jacket, then began to unknot his tie. It felt as though it was strangling him all of a sudden.

"Hey, wait a minute," she said. "I didn't say anything about the tie. People might get the wrong idea."

Even though he knew she was teasing, he felt the need to defend his attire. "I went straight from my meeting this morning in New York to the airport, and then straight from the airport here to the track. Haven't even checked into my hotel yet." He let out a sigh, feeling suddenly exhausted. "It's been a long day."

"And we've barely gotten started here. Better pace yourself, cowboy." She reached up to her hair, pushing a few damp tendrils away from her face. "Anyway, what's this about a business meeting? I thought you said you were retired from the finance biz."

"From fund management, yeah," he said with a nod. "But I'm still involved with my family's charitable foundation. Right now I'm dividing my time between New York and the winery."

"And races on the weekend?"

"For the next few months, at least."

Shelly nodded. "Sounds like you have a lot on your plate."

Damon just shrugged. "I like to keep busy."

"Yeah, me, too," she agreed.

"How do you do it?" he asked, unable to curb his curiosity. "I mean, being the only female driver in the series. That's got to be tough, right?"

"Well, there's plenty of wives and girlfriends around. It's not like I'm the only woman at the track."

"Yeah, but you're not one of them."

"Thanks for reminding me," she said with a grimace.

He shook his head. "I didn't mean it like that. Just that you're not a wife or girlfriend."

"How do you know I'm not?" she said archly. "Maybe I am."

Of course. It had never even occurred to him that she could be both a driver *and* a driver's girlfriend. "What I meant was that you're here at the track because it's your job," he clarified, feeling foolish. "Because you're a driver, not a driver's wife."

She smiled, her blue eyes dancing with mischief. "I knew what you meant. I was just giving you a hard time."

He cleared his throat uncomfortably. "I suppose if we're considering you for the sponsorship, we should probably know if you're currently involved with anyone. In NASCAR," he clarified.

"Hold on and let me find my list. It's pretty long. Sometimes I have a hard time keeping track." She pushed off the bar and took two steps away before stopping and turning back to face him. "Kidding. But you should have seen your face."

He couldn't help but laugh. "And here I thought I had the perfect poker face."

"Not by a long shot. And no, I'm not involved with anyone here at the track. Or anywhere else, for that matter. I did go out with Al's nephew for a few months last year, but it ended badly. *Really* badly, so don't mention it to Al or he'll start yelling at me again. And since we're being so open and honest, how about you?"

"What about me?"

"Are you involved with anyone?"

He shrugged. "Off and on for four years now."

"Uh-oh, a commitment phobe. Let me guess, your parents are divorced?"

He shook his head. "No, they've been happily married for more than forty years."

She looked genuinely surprised. "Really? Wow, that's a long time. Do you have any brothers or sisters?"

"One brother, three sisters. I'm the youngest."

Shelly sat perched on the edge of the couch now, just a couple of feet away from him. "Five kids? I can't even imagine. It must have been so…so *loud* growing up."

He laughed then, remembering the general happy chaos of his youth. "You have no idea. My grandmother lived with us, too."

"And your father did this hedge-fund thing, too? The banking stuff you do?"

He nodded. "It's a family business."

She leaned toward him, and he could definitely smell her shampoo now. Coconut, just like he'd thought. "So your brother, too?" she asked, and it took him a minute to remember the question.

"No, not Mario. Mario never had any interest in finance." Except his trust fund, of course. He was vastly interested in that, but Damon would never say that aloud.

"What about your sisters? Any of them in the family business? Or are girls not allowed?"

"Actually, my oldest sister Kate worked at TCM for a few years. Ran her own fund, and did really well, too. But then she got married, and she and her husband moved to Chicago. She works for a firm there, now. I guess none of the rest of them were interested." He paused, realizing the direction the conversation had taken. "Wait, why are we talking about my family?"

"I don't know," she answered with a shrug. "It just seemed more interesting than talking about me."

"Maybe from your perspective. But I'm supposed to be learning everything I can about you."

"Okay, okay," she conceded with a groan. She obviously hated talking about herself. "What else do you want to know?"

Business. He needed to get back to business. "What made you want to be a race-car driver?"

She reached down to scratch one ankle as she considered the question. "It's all I've ever wanted to be. I can't even imagine doing anything else. Well, except maybe being a mechanic or car engineer or something like that. I like to take things apart, and then put them back together again. Might have studied engineering if I'd gone to college. But like I said, my racing career took off really quickly, and I just never got around to it. I was a good student, though, in case you're wondering. I graduated at the top of my class."

Somehow, that didn't surprise him one bit. For a moment, he allowed himself to study her face. She was so different from the women he was used to, and yet there was a familiar quality to her, too. He couldn't quite figure it out. "But it couldn't have been easy," he said at last. "I mean, as a woman in a male-dominated sport, you must have—"

"Yoo-hoo," someone called out, just outside the door. "Open up, hon. My hands are full."

"Oh, no," Shelly whispered, the color visibly draining from her face as she stood.

Damon stood quickly, reaching for her arm. She looked as though she was going to faint. "What's wrong?"

"Everything," she murmured, her lips barely moving.

There was a loud rap and a scrape against the door, almost as if someone were kicking it. "C'mon, Shelly. I know you're in there."

"Who is that?" Damon asked.

"You've got to go," she whispered. "Now! C'mon, out the back door." Before he even had a chance to retrieve his jacket, she reached for his arm and started to tug him down the narrow hallway. They hadn't gotten far when the door banged open, revealing a woman standing on the steps who looked a lot like Shelly but with platinum hair, her roots several shades darker, her face lined with age.

"What're you doing just standing there with your mouth hanging open?" The woman turned and saw Damon standing there. "Ooh, sorry. I didn't realize you were entertainin'."

Shelly said nothing—she simply stared straight ahead, her cheeks stained a bright red.

"Well, c'mon, girl, aren't you goin' to introduce your momma to your handsome friend?"

"Damon," Shelly said, her voice flat, "meet my mother."

CHAPTER FOUR

SHELLY FELT AS IF SHE were going to be sick. How could she possibly have forgotten that she'd invited her mother to Daytona? The last time they'd spoken, Missy had sounded lonely, depressed. Shelly had felt bad; she hadn't seen her mother in months. So she'd asked her to come. She'd mentioned it to the team manager, and obviously someone had seen to the arrangements. But it had totally slipped her mind.

And now…here Missy was, in all her Spandex glory, batting her lashes at Damon Tieri—the very man who held Shelly's future in his hands. The man she was more than a little attracted to. The man she was kind of starting to like. The man who was maybe starting to like her a little bit, too.

This was bad. Very, very bad.

She watched in horror as Missy handed up a case of beer—a *case,* for God's sake. "Knew I'd have to bring my own," Missy said with a wink as Damon set it down next to the refrigerator. "Don't want to run out and have to pay track prices. Besides, they never have my favorite brand."

Shelly took a deep, gulping breath. She needed to do something. *Now.* But what? How could she possibly save the situation? She had to get rid of Damon, and fast. Only it was too late; Missy had already advanced on him.

"So, Damon, is it?" she was saying. "How long have you and my little girl—"

"No, Ma," Shelly interjected, panic making her heart race. "It's not like that. Damon's here on business. Racing business."

"That's a shame," Missy pouted. "'Course, my daughter has terrible taste in men. I should've known you were way too—"

"Damon was just leaving, Ma, so why don't you save it for later, okay?"

"I don't want to run him off, not if you've got business to do. Go on, don't mind me." Missy was raising her brows suggestively, tipping her head toward Damon in some strange pantomime. "I need to freshen up, anyway. It's hotter'n Hades out there and I'm sweating like a pig. Just let me get a beer, and I'll get out of your way."

"That's not necessary, Mrs. Green," Damon said, looking like a deer in headlights. "I've taken up too much of your daughter's time as it is. But it's good to meet you."

"Not half as good as it is to meet you," Missy answered with a leer, and Shelly groaned inwardly.

Damon smiled, nodding stiffly. She had to give him points for trying. "You must be very proud of Shelly. It's pretty amazing what she's accomplished."

Missy rolled her eyes in reply. "Well, it'd be even more amazing if she could manage to find herself a husband and settle down. You know, get herself a *real* job."

"I *do* have a real job," Shelly said through clenched teeth.

Missy laughed. "If you want to call it that."

"What did you have in mind instead?" Shelly snapped. "Flipping burgers at a fast-food place? Or bagging groceries at the Grocery Barn?"

"Sure put food on your table growing up, didn't it?" Missy shot back. "I didn't hear you complainin' then. Just because you think you're better than—"

"Enough, Ma. Okay? Please just let me show Damon out and then we can discuss career options all you like. C'mon." She gestured toward the door, terrified to meet his eyes, to see the horror she knew would be written all over his face.

Wordlessly, he retrieved his jacket from the couch and followed her out. Shelly slammed the door behind them, taking a deep, calming breath before she turned to face him. "I am *so* sorry about that. I totally forgot she was coming this weekend. I know she's a bit… much," she finished lamely.

"Don't worry about it," Damon said, then cleared his throat uncomfortably. "I…uh, I think I'll call it a day and head back to my hotel. But I'll be here all day tomorrow."

"Great. Maybe we can talk more then. I'd like to know a little more about the sponsorship—what kind of plans you have for marketing and all that." She was trying to sound professional, but it was hard with her mother not twenty feet away, probably watching them out the motor home's window.

"Of course," he said with a nod. "We'll talk more tomorrow."

Shelly swallowed hard. "Okay. Have a good night."

"You, too," he said, then turned and walked away, checking his watch as he went.

It was obvious that he was anxious to get away as fast as he could, and who could blame him? Missy sure knew how to clear a room, always did. She'd probably finished a six-pack before she'd arrived at the track. No doubt she'd be in rare form by tonight. Shelly dropped her head into her hands. This was not good, not good at all.

"GOOD MORNING," DAMON said, striding up behind Shelly. It was easy to spot her, what with the blond ponytail hanging out the back of her purple cap. "What's on tap for today?"

She spun around, looking surprised to see him there. She was wearing her ZippiPrint uniform, unzipped to the waist, the sleeves tied in the front. "Hi, there," she said, leaning back against the car, her cheeks flushed pink. "Good to see you again."

No doubt she was remembering her mother's appearance at the motor home yesterday. He wasn't quite sure what to say about it, or how to put her mind at ease. He'd lain awake half the night thinking about it, realizing the full extent of obstacles Shelly had faced to get where she was today. No wonder he hadn't talked to Steve about her. He didn't know what to say yet.

Obviously she hadn't gotten much support at home—a concept that was entirely foreign to him, but it seemed clear that her mother didn't seem to appreciate her daughter's success. He'd also been able to put two and two together regarding Al's comment about Shelly having good reason not to drink. Her mother traveled with a case of beer, after all.

While the businessman in him was horrified by the prospect of sponsoring a driver whose mother could very well prove to be an embarrassment to Pebble Valley Winery, the man inside him thought more highly of the woman who was able to overcome such limitations, to make so much of herself despite them. It couldn't have been an easy road for her.

"Damon?" she asked, drawing him out of his thoughts. "You okay?"

He snapped his attention back into focus, offering her what he hoped was an apologetic smile. "Sorry, I'm still a little tired, is all. Anyway, like I said, I'm kind of your shadow this weekend."

"Huh." She smiled up at him shyly. "I kind of thought that was just a figure of speech."

"No, I meant it literally. Well, almost literally. What's next on the schedule?"

"Qualifying at one. Two laps. Afterward, I'll probably hang out in my motor home and sign some stuff for Zippi-Print—that's part of the sponsorship deal, you know."

Damon shook his head. "I didn't know that."

"Then I think I've got a photo shoot at three. I hope it'll be quick—I hate that kind of thing. Hey, Al," she called out. "They're bringing someone to do hair and makeup and all that, aren't they?"

"Sure are," Al yelled back.

Shelly nodded. "Good. Anyway, after that, I've got the driver's meeting. When that's over, I've got a fan hospitality thing to go to. You know, a Q and A session, and then I'll sign stuff for a little bit. Then it's show time. One hundred laps. Two hundred and fifty miles."

"You've got all that to do today?" he asked. "I'm overwhelmed just listening to it. How do you keep it all straight?"

Shelly shrugged. "Thank goodness for Pam, my PR rep. She hands me a schedule, and then makes sure I'm where I need to be, when I need to be there. Like a baby-sitter. No way I could keep track of it all by myself. I'm too disorganized."

He couldn't help but smile. "Somehow I find that hard to believe."

Somewhere behind them, a cell phone rang. A minute later, Al strode into view, holding out the cell. "Shelly, it's Charlie. Got a sec?"

"Sure," she said, taking the phone and putting it to her ear.

Damon was pretty good with names, and he didn't remember meeting a Charlie. He wondered who he was, and what he was to Shelly.

"Hey, Charlie, what's going on? Oh, she's up already?" She glanced up at Damon, then took several steps away, her back toward him. She lowered her voice when she spoke next. "Yeah, sorry about that. Just make her something to eat, why don't you? Anything, doesn't matter, but try and stretch it out—you know, a nice, long meal. Keep her in the motor home, if you can." She shook her head. "I don't know, just talk real sweet to her like you always do."

Something Charlie said made her laugh. "Wait, I know, offer to bake cookies with her. You know, your famous peanut-butter cookies. She'll love that. Thanks, Charlie. I owe you big-time. Okay, I'll check in when I can, but I've got a busy day. Yeah, I know. Okay, thanks again. Bye."

Snapping shut the phone, she turned to glance at him sheepishly. "My mom," she said. "Poor Charlie's left to deal with her."

"And Charlie would be?" he prodded.

"My motor-home driver. He's a great guy, a retired fighter pilot. Anyway, it's about time to head down for qualifying." She untied the sleeves of her uniform and shrugged into them, then pulled the zipper up to her throat. "You coming?"

"I'm coming," he agreed with a nod, checking his watch. "Isn't it a little early, though? I thought you said one o'clock."

She smiled up at him. "Yeah, but you'll see why. Hey, it's kind of cool to have an extra shadow," she said as he fell into step beside her. "A girl could get used to this."

Out into the crowded throng of people they went, through the garage area and toward the pits. Every few minutes, someone stopped Shelly, handing her a hat or die-cast car or a shirt to sign. A few people asked to have their picture taken with her, and Damon obliged, acting as photographer as Shelly mugged it up with ecstatic fans decked out in colorful NASCAR gear.

For a second there, Damon glanced down at his own boring khakis and polo shirt and decided he should hit the merchandise haulers later on. *When in Rome*...he told himself, watching as Shelly stopped to chat with yet another group of race fans wearing the blue and yellow colors of Trey Sanford's sponsor, Greenstone Garden Centers.

Damon was amazed at her ease with fans. She had a ready smile for everyone. And it was more than that, she actually listened to what they had to say, asked questions about where they were from, how they were enjoying themselves at the track. There was no glancing over her shoulder, acting like she had somewhere to be. No wonder she was so popular.

Eventually the crowd thinned as they continued on their way. "Okay, now I see why we had to leave so early," he said, shaking his head in amazement.

"Knew you would." Her smile was one of smug satisfaction.

"Don't you ever get tired of it? Chatting and smiling and signing things, I mean."

"No way. That's half the fun. Anyway, these folks spend their hard-earned money to come out here and support us, week after week. The least we can do is show them some love, right?"

"Look, Daddy! There she is! It's Shelly Green," a

voice squealed, and Shelly and Damon turned toward it. A man stood with two small, dark-haired girls on the other side of a chain-link fence. They were identical twins, about six or seven, Damon would guess. He had nieces about their age.

"Hey, there," Shelly called out, headed their way with Damon trailing behind. "Wow, I like your shirts," she said.

Both girls wore green ZippiPrint Racing shirts, a purple No. 411 in the middles of their small chests.

"Would you like me to sign them?" Shelly offered, whipping out a black marker. "I always carry an extra one, just in case," she whispered in Damon's ear.

"That would be great," the dad said, looking entirely dazzled and starstruck. "They're big fans of yours. Came today just to see you race."

"Well, then, I'll try and race really well today, just for you two. What're your names?" she asked, gesturing for the dad to lift them so she could reach over the fence to sign the shirts.

"I'm Kaylie," the girl being lifted said, "and this is Kristen." She pointed to her twin still on the ground, looking up wide-eyed at Shelly. "I'm the older one," she added proudly.

Shelly laughed, scribbling her name on the girl's shoulder. "Oh, yeah? How much older? A minute?"

"Six minutes," the one called Kristen said, rolling her eyes. "And she thinks that means she can boss me around."

The dad lowered the first girl and raised the second one for Shelly's marker. "We really appreciate this," he said. "I think you've probably made their year."

"Hey, no problem. I'm really glad to meet y'all. Us girls got to stick together, right? So, what do you two want to be when you grow up?"

"Race-car drivers, just like you," the pair said in unison.

"Yeah?" Shelly scribbled her name a second time. "Well, you have to work really, really hard. And do well in school, too," she added, winking at their father. "Probably best to go to college first. Get a degree in engineering or something."

The girls just nodded. The father looked just as dumbstruck as his children. Probably that wink, Damon realized. She'd stunned the poor man, probably temporarily stopped his heart. She seemed to have no idea of the effect she had on men.

"Well, I've got to get to qualifying," Shelly said, handing Damon the marker. "You'll be watching, right?"

"We sure will," they said.

"I'll wave!" the girl on the right said.

"I'll wave back, right when I cross the start/finish line, okay? You watch for it."

Again, they nodded solemnly.

"Is that guy your boyfriend?" the girl on the left asked, pointing at Damon.

At once, Shelly's cheeks flooded with color as she shook her head. "No, he's, um, just a business associate," she stammered. "That's all."

The look of relief on the father's face was unmistakable. A single dad, perhaps? Whatever the case, a jolt of jealousy shot through Damon, taking him entirely by surprise.

"I better go," Shelly said, waving good-bye.

"Bye, Shelly," the kids called out after her. "Good luck!"

Damon fell into step beside her as they continued on toward pit road, an uncomfortable silence between them now.

What the hell had just happened? Of course he was just a business associate. Not only that, but they'd only recently met. He barely knew her. What's more, Shelly wasn't at all his type. Not that it mattered, since he was involved with someone else.

And yet, as completely illogical as it was, disappointment had shot through him when she'd denied that he was anything more to her than exactly what he was— a business associate. A casual acquaintance.

But damn if he didn't wish he were more than that.

SHELLY REACHED FOR another ZippiPrint hat, trying to ignore the cramp in her hand. She'd had four boxes of them brought to her motor home. She had an hour till the photo shoot; she figured she could knock out a couple hundred of them in that time.

Of course, she hadn't counted on Damon coming back with her after qualifying. He was really taking this whole 'shadow' thing seriously.

Not that she minded, really, except that Missy was there, too. Supposedly staying out of their way, but every once in a while she had to pop in and say something wildly inappropriate, as was her habit. At least she'd ditched the Spandex today for a pair of jeans. If it wasn't for the T-shirt that was way too tight and low-cut for a woman her age, she'd almost pass for normal.

"Ready for me to open the next box?" Damon asked.

"Sure. I'm almost done with this one."

"Anyway, only a couple of California wineries produce a white Merlot," he continued, picking up the thread of conversation from before their last interruption. He loved to talk about wine, and Shelly wanted to learn as much as she could, and quickly.

"Is that anything like White Zinfandel?" she asked.

He nodded. "Very similar, though it's a little more full-bodied. It's particularly popular with female drinkers, and that's a demographic I'd like to do better with. I think it's a market that Pebble Valley can compete in, and compete well."

"Sounds like a good idea," she murmured, flexing her fingers. "Particularly with the NASCAR connections. They say nearly half the sport's fans are women now. Were you planning any television spots? Lots of funny commercials run during races, advertising sponsors' products."

"I think we will, eventually. I'll probably stay away from funny, though. Just doesn't jive with our image. It'll have to be something more sophisticated."

She looked up from the hat in her hand, shaking her head. "I don't know, Tieri. Everyone really likes the funny ones."

He just shrugged, ripping off the tape sealing one of the boxes. "Kyle Markham is truly a gifted winemaker. Steve and I think Pebble Valley has the potential to become a household name, with some targeted promotion. The winery is starting to get noticed in the industry, especially for our Sauvignon blanc. Ours has really exceptional fresh, floral notes. Incidentally, Sauvignon blanc is another variety popular with female drinkers."

"What about sparkling wines?" Shelly asked. "You know, like champagne?"

"Well, that's a whole different process. It's—ouch!"

"What'd you do?" Shelly asked, peering over the pile of hats beside her.

"Paper cut. Cardboard cut, actually. I better get a paper towel before I bleed all over your floor."

"Here, let me do it." Shelly set aside her marker and hurried into the galley kitchen. She grabbed an entire roll of paper towels off the counter and dashed back. "Let me see it," she said, reaching for his hand. Tiny droplets of crimson blood welled on the edge of his palm, just below his little finger. "I should probably get you some antiseptic for that."

"No, it's fine." He dabbed at it with a wadded-up paper towel. "Look, it's stopping bleeding already."

He was right. "Guess you're not much of a bleeder, huh? Want me to kiss it and make it better?" she teased, raising his hand to her lips.

It felt like an electric shock went through her body, raising gooseflesh on her arms. He must have felt it, too, because he looked down at her strangely, as if startled.

For several seconds, neither of them spoke. They simply stood there, Shelly still holding his hand in her own.

"Am I interrupting anything?" Missy chirped, breaking the silence.

Shelly guiltily dropped his hand, feeling foolish. "No, Ma. What do you need?"

"I think Trixie's got to go. Poor thing's crossing her little legs back there. I'd take her out myself, but I'm watching my stories. I tape 'em all week, and catch up on weekends," she directed at Damon, who still hadn't managed to say anything.

"No problem," Shelly said through clenched teeth. "I'll take her out. I was just about done signing stuff, anyway."

"Oh, and when you go out, do you think you could get me a beer? I'm all out. I'll bet you Charlie raided my stash. You better watch that one," she warned, wagging a finger.

Shelly tried not to groan aloud as she watched Missy sashay back to the bedroom. If she could make it through the weekend without strangling her mother, it would be a small miracle.

Truth was, she didn't want her mom to ruin things. She liked Damon. A lot. And not just as some business associate—not just a guy she had to impress to win a sponsorship. She wanted to impress him as a *woman*. That realization shocked the hell out of her, mostly because it was so out of character for her.

But then again, he was handsome, successful and kind of funny, too, in a self-deprecating way that she found appealing. And there was definitely some physical chemistry between them—that little electrical jolt wasn't just her imagination. It had been real, and she was pretty sure he'd felt it, too.

She'd have to be crazy *not* to want him, she told

herself. So what if he was a little stiff? Nobody was perfect. Heaven knows, she wasn't. Still, the idea that she was interested in him as a man made her feel weird, kind of awkward. It was out of her comfort zone, somewhere she rarely ventured.

"Let's go walk the dog," Damon said behind her.

"Yep," Shelly said, unable to turn around and face him lest he see how flushed her cheeks were. "I'll go get the leash."

CHAPTER FIVE

DAMON SLID INTO THE booth opposite Shelly, Adam Sanford beside her.

"We need some champagne," Sanford said, taking the menu the hostess offered. "This is a celebration."

Beside him, Shelly smiled. "My first win at Daytona," she said, tossing her ponytail. "I can barely believe it. Daytona, Loudon and 'Dega, all in one season."

"And it's not even over yet," Sanford reminded her.

"So where does that put you in points?" Damon asked.

"Still second place, but we're only fifteen points out now. I can almost *taste* a championship. 'Course, there's still a lot of the season left, but I'd say we're definitely on the right track."

Sanford clapped her on the shoulder. "She's pretty amazing, isn't she? I'd love to see her in a Sprint Cup car."

Damon nodded in agreement. "I admit, I'm impressed." Very impressed. He'd seen enough racing over the course of the last few days to know that Shelly had talent—serious talent.

But there was more to it than that. He couldn't even imagine what it must have been like for Shelly, growing up with that mother of hers. The more he watched them together, the more obvious it became that Shelly was the caretaker, more adult than Missy was. How Shelly became so successful with those kind of disadvantages, he couldn't imagine.

But she had. By all accounts, Shelly was universally well-respected, the consummate professional. Her work ethic was near legendary, and it was something with which he readily identified. Hard work, dedication to the point of tunnel vision—that was what had made him a successful fund manager, what had earned him his fortune.

Of course, he'd also had advantages—a supportive family, too supportive, perhaps. Money. Education. Tradition. He'd simply followed in his father's footsteps, joining a family business that was already well established and reputable. He'd always done exactly what was expected of him, followed the path his parents had laid out for his life.

Shelly had none of that. Everything she'd accomplished had been accomplished on her own merit, as a result of her own doing. And damn if he didn't admire the hell out of that.

He glanced across the table at her while she studied the menu, chewing thoughtfully on her lower lip.

"Mmm, the braised ribs sound good," she murmured, turning toward Adam Sanford. "What were you thinking, boss?"

"I was thinking steak. Damon?"

"The salmon sounds good," Damon answered with a shrug.

"Oh, no," Shelly said with a sigh. "Please don't tell me you're one of those guys who doesn't eat meat."

Damon shook his head. "I grew up in an Italian-American household with a grandma who loved to cook. Trust me, I eat plenty of meat."

"Well, thank goodness for that. My granny always said you should never trust a man who doesn't eat meat."

"Interesting. And why is that?"

Shelly shrugged. "I have no idea. Of course, she also always said that a lady never leaves her house without lipstick on, and I never much listened to that. 'Course, I never much considered myself a lady, either," she finished with a grin.

Damon resisted the urge to lean across the table and inhale Shelly's sweet coconut scent. Thank God her mother had left right after the celebration in Victory Lane had ended. Shelly deserved to celebrate, not make more arrangements to keep her mother out of trouble. Without that added responsibility, she seemed as if a huge weight had been lifted from her shoulders.

Her *bare* shoulders, he mentally added. Other than that one time in her motor home, she'd been wearing her racing uniform every time he'd seen her at the track. Seeing her now in a halter top and jeans was somehow disorienting, he realized, forcing his gaze away from the broad expanse of bare skin and up to her face, instead.

Her big blue eyes met his, and she smiled. "So," she said, oozing confidence, "let's talk about that sponsorship deal."

"Let the man order his dinner first, Shel," Sanford chastised, then signaled their waiter.

As soon as they'd ordered, Shelly tried again. "Okay, can we talk about the sponsorship now? I'd really like to know your thoughts—"

"I'd really rather not," Damon said, shifting uncomfortably in his seat. He'd already gone over his and Steve's initial plan with her, outlining the responsibilities they'd expect from their driver. Couldn't she just enjoy herself tonight? "This is supposed to be a celebratory dinner, not a business meeting. There's plenty of time—"

"Why wait?" she pressed. "I want to strike while the iron is hot."

"Right now I'm just trying to wrap my head around the sport, to get to know *several* drivers personally. There's not much more to discuss at this point."

"Uh-oh," Sanford muttered, glancing down at his vibrating cell phone. "I gotta take this." He scooted out of the booth and headed toward the hostess stand, walking out into the restaurant's lobby.

"Wonder what that's about," Shelly said, then shrugged, turning her attention back to Damon. "Anyway, what were we talking about? Oh, yeah. The sponsorship," she said, as if she had forgotten. "I know you've been asking around about me. Just so you know, Al can't keep a secret."

He took a deep breath before he spoke, carefully measuring his words. "There's no doubt in my mind that you're one of the best drivers in the series, Shelly. But there's a little more to our decision than that."

Shelly shook her head. "I don't see why. Pebble Valley should want the best. And I'm the best, Damon."

Mercifully, Sanford took that moment to reappear at the table. "I'm sorry, Shelly, but I've got to go. I hate to abandon you like this, but it can't wait."

"That's okay," Shelly said. "Hey, I hope it's nothing serious."

"Nah." He waved one hand in dismissal. "Just something I have to see to personally. I gave the waiter my credit-card number. Stay, have dessert. Don't feel like you have to rush, okay?"

"Gotcha," Shelly said. "Anyway, you know I never turn down dessert."

"We'll speak later," Sanford directed at him, and Damon just nodded.

"Well, that's too bad," Shelly said as Sanford hurried out. "What do you suppose we should do with his dinner?"

"Might as well get it wrapped up. I bet someone back at the track will take it off your hands."

"Yeah, I guess I can give it to Charlie."

"Charlie?" he asked. "Wait, the motor-home driver?"

"Yeah, and sometimes cook. I don't know what I'd do without him."

"It would seem that most of the people you work with are pretty devoted to you," Damon said, eyeing her curiously. "Almost religiously, even."

"It's that Southern charm of mine, I guess," she drawled. "Plus, I can make a mean pot roast."

"Really?" he asked, unable to hide his surprise.

Her mouth curved into a grin. "No. Not really. But did you have to look *so* shocked?"

The waiter reappeared carrying an ice bucket and two glass flutes. "Champagne," he announced, setting the glasses in front of them. "And your food will be right out. Enjoy." He filled both flutes and set the bottle back in the bucket before disappearing.

Damon watched Shelly eye her glass warily, indecision flitting across her features. Finally, she reached for the flute and tipped it to her lips, taking a small sip. "It's good," she murmured, even while her face twisted with obvious distaste.

"You don't have to drink it for my benefit," he said. "Al already told me—"

"Told you what?" she interrupted, her eyes widening.

"Just that you're not much of a drinker."

A flush stained Shelly's cheeks red. "I have been known to have a glass of champagne now and then."

Damon narrowed his eyes, taken slightly aback by her outburst.

"Look, I realize that I'm not…classy, or sophisticated, or whatever you want to call it. I'm a race-car driver, and I make no apologies for it. I'm sure I'm nothing like your girlfriend—"

"You and Courtney come from totally different backgrounds," he said with a shrug, "but you're actually more alike than you'd expect. You're both successful women, good at what you do."

"And let me guess…she's Ivy League like you?"

He shook his head. "Nope, Wellesley, actually."

"Well, I bet her family is as blue-blooded as yours."

"I wouldn't exactly call my family blue-blooded. Successful, yes. But my grandfather was an immigrant from Italy, and my father is a self-made man. We Tieris know the value of hard work."

"Managing rich people's money. That *is* what you do, isn't it? I know how to do an Internet search," she added, her blush deepening.

"Do you have a problem with that?"

Leaning her elbows on the table, Shelly shrugged. "It's just that those Wall Street types seem so out of touch with the rest of society. It's really all about money for them, isn't it?"

"Unlike those NASCAR types?" he quipped. "You get compensated pretty generously, wouldn't you say?"

Before Shelly could respond, the waiter reappeared with their food. Neither spoke a word as they accepted their steaming plates. The waiter must have noticed the tension hanging heavy in the air, because he scurried away as fast as possible, leaving them both glaring at one another across the width of the table.

"A lot of the funds I manage belong to charitable trusts," Damon said at last, breaking the uncomfortable silence. "I promise you, it isn't all about greed."

"Do you have any idea how much the NASCAR community gives to charity each year?" Shelly countered. "Or how many hours we devote to charitable causes? And not because we have to, but because we *want* to?"

"So you're saying that NASCAR contributes more to

the greater good of society than Wall Street? Exactly how many Wall Street types do you know?"

"Just one, and he's irritating the hell out of me right now."

"Maybe we should eat our dinner and leave philosophical debates for later."

"What, you think I can't keep up? Try me."

"Your mind is plenty sharp, Shelly. I wish I'd thought to wear my body armor."

She smiled at that, one cheek dimpling. "Actually, I kind of like arguing with you."

"Yeah?"

"Yeah. You get this puffed-up look about you. I think you need to loosen up some, Tieri. Maybe you should finish off that champagne. That'll help."

"Actually, champagne just gives me a headache. Unless it's Cristal, of course."

"Of course," Shelly said with a shrug. "That's why I insist on it in Victory Lane. Spray me with anything else, and I get mad as a hornet."

"Are hornets really that mad? I've always wondered."

"Obviously you've never met one. Guess they don't have 'em much on Park Avenue, huh?"

"Fifth," he corrected.

"Right. The best address. I forgot. So tell me, Tieri, what do you drive? Or *do* you drive? I guess you could just take a cab everywhere. Or a limo."

"I drive. And very well, thank you."

"You didn't answer my question."

He picked up his fork. "Eat your dinner, it's getting cold."

Shelly rolled her eyes. "You sound like Charlie. You know, he actually cuts my crusts off my sandwiches? And then he slices them into little triangles. You'd think I was five."

"Maybe because you sometimes act like you're five?" he ventured, mostly trying to distract her.

"You still didn't answer my question. Which means you're avoiding it. Which means you drive something really ostentatious. A convertible?" she guessed. "No?" she asked when he didn't reply. "More embarrassing than that? A luxury sedan? Please don't say it's an Italian sportscar. If it is, I'll have to stage an intervention, you know."

He laid down his fork and met her amused gaze. "A station wagon."

She laughed so loudly that several nearby diners turned to stare. "You drive a station wagon?" she finally choked out.

It *was* pretty funny, actually. "It's a very safe car," he said with mock seriousness. "Reliable, too."

"Who are you, my granny? How's that salmon, by the way?"

"I don't know." He pushed it around his plate. "I haven't managed to get a bite in yet."

"Sorry," she said with a wince. "Didn't mean to distract you."

"No, it was well worth it." He couldn't remember when he'd had such fun. Shelly made him laugh, something Courtney rarely accomplished, despite her education and perfect pedigree.

"It *is* getting late, though," he said. "We probably should eat and get out of here."

"Yeah, I guess you're right," she conceded. "We're not going to talk about the sponsorship, are we?"

He shook his head. "Sorry. We're supposed to be celebrating, remember?"

"Crap." She actually reached for her champagne and took another sip. "Okay, I'll eat. Uh-oh, I just realized that Adam took the car. You'll have to give me a ride back to the track."

"That's okay. It'll just give us more time to *not* talk about the sponsorship."

"I'm beginning to think you like to torture me," she said, wrinkling her nose. Her adorable nose, he amended. Sprinkled with freckles that she didn't hide with makeup.

He clenched his hands into fists, resisting the urge to reach across the table and trace the freckles with his finger.

She's the one torturing me, he realized with a start.

CHAPTER SIX

AS SHE FOLLOWED DAMON across the streetlamp-lit parking lot, Shelly inhaled deeply, filling her lungs with the warm, salt-scented air. Beyond the asphalt, beige sand stretched out to the ocean's edge where the tips of rolling waves were illuminated by silvery moonlight.

"I love Daytona," she said, turning her face toward the crashing waves. "One of these days I'd like to spend an entire week here, just lounging on the beach."

"It *is* beautiful, isn't it?" Damon asked, pausing by a red rental sedan. For a full half minute, he gazed out at the ocean, the breeze ruffling his dark hair. When he turned back toward her, his face was lit with a smile. "Are you in any rush to get back to the track?"

"What did you have in mind?" she countered with a grin.

He shrugged, shoving his hands into his pockets. "A walk on the beach, maybe?"

Shelly tried not to laugh. "In those shoes?" She was willing to bet they were Italian. Probably cost a couple of hundred bucks a pair.

He scowled at her. "I was planning on taking them off. If you're game, that is."

"Sure, why not?" Shelly answered, hating the way her heart leapt in response to his invitation. After all, he'd only asked her to go for a walk—nothing too illicit in that.

She followed him down the length of the lot and over the curb to a sidewalk that ran parallel to the shore. As soon as they reached the sand's edge, they both stopped to remove their shoes. "Think it's okay just to leave them here?" she asked.

"Probably. We won't be too long." He started off toward the crashing waves, Shelly hurrying to keep pace. "I'll get you back to the track before you turn into a pumpkin, I promise."

"Cinderella and I don't have much in common," Shelly muttered. "No Prince Charming in sight, for one."

At that his mouth curved into a smile, but he said nothing. Once he reached the water's edge, he paused, staring out at the inky horizon. Shelly joined him, wrapping her arms around herself. "I've always dreamed of owning a beach house. Doesn't have to be big or fancy or anything. Maybe someday…" she trailed off, tracing an arc in the wet sand with her big toe.

"Here in Florida?" Damon asked.

"Nah. Maybe the Outer Banks. Wouldn't make much sense now, though. I travel too much."

"Yeah, you don't get much time off, do you?"

"No, but that's okay. I do love the ocean, though."

"Me, too," he said, shoving his hands into his pockets. "Growing up, I spent every summer at the beach."

"Really?"

He nodded. "My family has a summer house on the

Vineyard. Up island, near Aquinnah," he added, as if that meant anything to her.

"So in plain English, that would mean what?" she asked, shaking her head.

"What? Oh, up island? That's the far western part of the Vineyard. It's not as toney as, say, Vineyard Haven, but it's quieter and you can't beat the views from the bluffs."

"Is the house right on the ocean?"

"On a rocky cliff overlooking it. There's a path going down, pretty treacherous, too. I remember cracking my head open on the slippery rocks once or twice as a kid. Just about gave my mother a heart attack."

"I can only imagine," Shelly said with a laugh.

"Anyway, the views are incredible."

Shelly closed her eyes, inhaling deeply. "Describe it. The house, I mean. Everything."

He shook his head. "Nah, it's pretty boring. Just your average beach house. More like a cottage, really."

Her eyes flew open. "No, I really want to hear about it. Please?"

"Well, okay. Let's see…I guess it's what they call Craftsman style." He paused a beat. "You know, sort of blends in with the surroundings? Lots of wood, beamed ceilings. The entire back wall is pretty much all glass, and every room has an ocean view."

"And outside?" Shelly prodded.

"There's tall sea grass all around, and the cliff face is craggy, the rocks a deep red. The surf is pretty rough around there, but our beach is a little crescent cove, protected on three sides. It's great for kids, pretty shallow, with tidal pools on each end."

"I can totally envision it," Shelly breathed. "It sounds perfect." She opened her eyes, surprised to find that Damon had moved closer—so close she could smell his masculine scent. He smelled like no one she knew, like expensive cologne and some other scent she couldn't identify, but which reminded her of sunshine.

"Perfect," Damon murmured, so close now that their shoulders brushed.

The surf rushed in, cold across Shelly's ankles, but that wasn't what made her shudder. It was Damon, his closeness. He leaned in, his gaze locked on her lips, as if…as if he was going to kiss her.

His dark eyes reflected the moon, and Shelly's breath hitched in her chest as his lips came closer. Her own lips parted in surprise, her eyes closing instinctively as his hands cupped her face, his breath warm against her cheek.

When his lips finally touched hers, a shiver worked its way down her spine. His kiss was tender at first, just a feather-light pressure, nipping and retreating. Shelly moaned softly, unable to bear the sweetness of it. And then his kiss grew more fierce, his lips nearly crushing hers.

Rising on tiptoe, Shelly wrapped her hands around his neck, tangling her fingers in his hair as she pressed herself against him, opening her mouth against his.

Good grief, how long had it been since she'd been kissed like this? She couldn't remember, couldn't think, could barely feel the waves lapping at her ankles, her feet sinking into the warm, wet sand as the kiss went on and on. Dang it if her head didn't start to spin, her legs growing strangely weak.

"I'm sorry," he murmured, his mouth leaving her lips. "I probably shouldn't have done that." His lips were warm against her neck now, raising gooseflesh on her skin. He found the spot beneath her ear where her pulse fluttered like butterfly wings, his tongue drawing slow, lazy circles against her skin.

"No, but I'm glad you did," Shelly said, tipping her head back, breathless now.

A wave crashed behind them, the only sound save the beating of Shelly's heart—a loud, deafening din. Shelly wondered if Damon could hear it, too.

"I don't think I've ever met anyone quite like you, Shelly Green," Damon said, his voice soft.

Shelly's eyes fluttered open at last. They stood, clutched in an embrace for several seconds, saying nothing. Shelly concentrated on regulating her breathing, on calming her racing heart, but it was impossible with him so close.

He was like her, she realized, feeling a surprising camaraderie with him. Driven, determined. When he set his mind to something, he accomplished it. She had no doubt that he'd make Pebble Valley Winery a huge success. Heck, by the end of the season, he'd probably be fully qualified to run a NASCAR team. Because, like her, when he set out to do something, he did it well.

Including kiss. He definitely excelled at that, she decided.

Voices carried on the breeze, laughing, growing

closer. They were no longer alone, there on the moonlit beach. The spell broken, they stepped apart just as a pair of teenagers strolled past, hand in hand.

"Wow," Shelly said, trying to regain her balance in the wet sand. Feeling almost shy, she tentatively raised her gaze, searching his expression. He looked...*regretful,* she realized. That he had kissed her? Or that they had been interrupted?

"I should get you back to the track," he said, reaching for her hand.

"Probably so," she muttered, silently cursing the intruders. Which was stupid, really, because she knew she probably should have been thanking them.

Damon's face was unreadable as he led her back to the parking lot. Which was a good thing, Shelly realized. There was no telling what was going through his head. Several options popped into her mind, none of them pleasant.

The only thing Shelly was sure of was that she'd never felt so dangerously attracted to anyone before. No man's kiss had ever affected her as Damon's had, leaving her breathless and disoriented—and aching for more.

They'd reached the sidewalk where their shoes still lay, undisturbed. Damon released her hand at last, and an empty feeling washed over her.

Snap out of it, she scolded herself as she wiped off her sandy feet and shoved them into her ballet flats. Following Damon to his rental car, she silently swore that she was going to *kill* Adam Sanford for dragging Damon along tonight, and then leaving her alone with him. Not because she hadn't enjoyed herself—oh no, to the contrary, she'd enjoyed herself way *too* much.

But because now she was even more confused than ever. She had confirmation that her attraction wasn't one-sided, that he was feeling something, too. But the question remained—what were they going to do about it?

July, Joliet, Illinois

AL SCRIBBLED SOME NOTES on his clipboard, glancing up when Shelly walked into the garage stall. His brow furrowed at once. "Hey, Shel, you look pale. You all right?"

Shelly zipped up her uniform and fastened the tab at her throat. "Just tired, is all. Didn't sleep well last night."

"Well, you've got practice in half an hour. After that, take a nap or something, why don't you?"

"Maybe I will." She could use a nap. Truth was, she'd been restless all week. She'd been an idiot to kiss Damon in Daytona, and even more of an idiot to have let it affect her the way it had. In all likelihood, he'd probably pushed it from his mind entirely, while she kept going over the night in question, replaying everything over and over again in her head.

Especially the kiss. There was no denying that the kiss had been one of the day's highlights, second only to her trip to Victory Lane. She tried to remind herself that she was a big girl—that they'd simply given in to a magical moment there in the moonlight, that it didn't have to mean anything. This wasn't high school; you didn't kiss a guy and then start going steady. It didn't work that way with adults. Things just…happened sometimes.

But the truth was, she wanted it to mean something. They hadn't talked about it—maybe that's what was bothering her, she realized. The drive back to the track afterward had been a little awkward, and neither of them had said much.

Not that Damon hadn't been a perfect gentleman. When they'd reached the track, he'd jumped out and hurried around the car to open the door for her—something she wasn't at all used to—and then he had insisted on walking her to the motor-home lot.

When they'd reached her place, he'd paused, taking her hand in his. Leaning against the aluminum siding, he'd stared down at her, that same heated look in his gaze as before, and for a second there Shelly had thought he was going to kiss her again. Her heart had begun to race in anticipation, her legs growing weak and rubbery.

But then Charlie had burst out with Trixie on her leash, nearly scaring them both half to death, and that had been the end of it. Damon had said a quick goodbye, and she hadn't heard from him since. Not that she'd expected to. Still…

"Hey, did you hear that Tieri's here?" Al asked. "Yeah," he continued when Shelly just stood there gaping. "He's a guest of Kyle Jordan's this time. Looks like you've got some competition, huh?"

"I guess I do," she muttered, trying to hide her surprise. To be fair, Damon had said he was going to take his time, get to know the sport, and meet several drivers personally before he made his decision. It made sense that he'd consider Kyle Jordan—he was the current points leader, a series favorite, and he was definitely looking for a NASCAR Sprint Cup Series ride. He was also an egotistical jerk, but Damon could figure that out for himself.

In the meantime, she'd just play it cool. Pretend the kiss hadn't happened, if that was how he wanted it. She could be nonchalant. Mature. Unruffled. Couldn't she?

Oh, yeah. As cool as a cucumber.

"Hey, Green," a voice behind her called, and she turned toward it with a start. *Speak of the devil.* Kyle Jordan, with Damon trailing behind him, a cell phone to his ear.

"How's the restoration project coming along?" Kyle asked, stepping into the garage's shade.

"Pretty good, thanks." That car was her baby—a '59 250GT coupe that had needed some serious work when she'd bought it last winter. She was restoring it, taking the time to do it right.

"Mind if I stop by sometime and have a look?" Jordan asked.

Shelly shrugged, forcing her gaze to remain on Jordan and not the man behind him flipping shut his phone. "Sure, anytime," she said with a smile. "You know where to find me."

"I don't know why you bothered with that house in Mooresville," Jordan ribbed her. "From what I hear, you might as well just put a cot at the shop."

"Yeah, thanks for reminding me that I have no life."

"You said it, not me. Hey, you know Damon Tieri, right? Steve Clayton's new partner at the winery?"

Damon had finally stepped up and joined them, wearing a pair of rumpled khakis and a forest-green polo shirt emblazoned with the Pebble Valley Winery logo. He looked hot and tired and a little disheveled and…well, *hot.* It was hard to think of him as anything but, try as she might.

"Yeah, Tieri and I go way back," she said at last, boldly meeting his gaze.

"Really?" Jordan's brow was furrowed in confusion. He wouldn't know a joke if it smacked him upside the head.

Shelly couldn't help but roll her eyes. "No, not really. But yeah, we've already met."

His eyes never leaving hers, Damon held out his hand. "Nice to see you again, Shelly." He looked so serious, so earnest. What did that mean?

"Yeah, you, too," she muttered as she took his hand and shook it.

"Shelly!" Al bellowed behind her. "It's about that time. C'mon, don't let the dust settle."

She turned toward her crew chief who was exaggeratedly pointing to his watch.

With a nod, Shelly turned back toward Jordan and Damon. "Well, guys, I guess I'd better—"

The garage stall was empty. A sudden heat flooded her cheeks as she watched the pair walk off through the crowd without a backward glance. Apparently she'd been dismissed, just like that.

Anger and embarrassment jockeyed for position in her mind. Luckily, anger won out. Once and for all, she would settle this. She would show Damon who the better driver was, who deserved the sponsorship. After this weekend, there would be no doubt in his mind.

She was going to outrace Kyle Jordan, and have fun doing it, too. And as to their personal relationship, hers and Damon's…well, that would have to sort itself out. She couldn't let herself lose focus, not in the middle of the season, not when she was so close to making it big. Racing was her number-one priority. Winning. A NASCAR Sprint Cup ride was the prize, not Damon Tieri.

I've got to remember that.

"Let's get this show on the road," she called out, giving Al the thumbs-up as she strode confidently to her car and climbed inside. She could do this—she knew she could. When she really wanted something, she always managed to get it. This sponsorship deal wouldn't be any different.

But Damon…that was a whole different story.

CHAPTER SEVEN

A BEAD OF SWEAT TRICKLED down the side of Shelly's face as she fought the wheel, struggling to keep the nose of her car out of the wall. Two car lengths ahead, Kyle Jordan hugged the low groove as he rocketed into Turn Two.

Not taking her eyes off Jordan's bumper, Shelly keyed her mike. "How are we on fuel, Al?"

"If we stay green to the end, we can make it," came Al's voice in reply. "Two, maybe three laps to spare."

"How about Jordan?"

"About the same. You've got sixteen laps to catch him. C'mon, little chickadee. Fly."

Damn it. No way was she letting him win this race, not today. Not with Damon up on Jordan's hauler, watching. Her car was tight, fighting her every step of the way, but it was fast, too. If she could just get around Jordan and get into that clean air up front, she could win this thing. Her car was better today, there was no doubt about it. They'd had one bad pit stop, just enough to lose the lead. It was her job to get it back.

She went hard on the throttle in the straightaway, the sun glancing off the blue bumper of Jordan's car as she closed the distance between them. As they headed into Turn One, the nose of her car inched up toward the back of Jordan's on the outside, causing his car to wiggle.

He was loose and getting looser as he struggled to maintain the lead, moving up across the track to block her as they headed into turn three.

"C'mon," Shelly muttered to herself, still fighting the steering wheel. Her shoulders ached with the effort, pain beginning to radiate down her arms.

Jordan blocked every move she made. When she dove low, he followed suit, his left side dipping down to the line. When she went high, he shot back up the track, the tail end of his car edging up toward the wall.

"Give it up, Jordan," she said through clenched teeth. He was too loose—he was going to wreck himself if he didn't let her by. There was no way he could block every line, and it was stupid of him to keep trying.

Three laps later, her patience was wearing thin. Her radio remained silent, her focus riveted on the car in front of her as she gave it one more try. It was time to get aggressive—if he wasn't going to move, she was going to have to give him a little help.

As they headed into Turn Three, she dropped to the inside line, waiting for the block. When it came, she accelerated, giving his bumper a tap, hoping to slide him up the track just enough for her to get by.

Instead, the nose of his car swung around, right into her path with a jarring impact. Next thing she knew, she was spinning, trying her best to hold on to the car as they slid down the track and into the grass.

After what felt like forever, her car came to rest against a barrier with a thud.

"You okay, Shelly?" came Al's worried voice.

Shelly opened her mouth to answer, but the breath was knocked from her lungs. For a few terrifying moments, she gasped for air, feeling suddenly sick to her stomach. Several seconds passed in tense silence.

"I'm okay, Al," she finally managed to choke out.

"Thank God," came his relieved voice. "You sure, though? That was a hard hit."

"Yeah, I'm sure," she gasped. "Sorry about that, guys." Her fingers shaking, she unbuckled her seat restraints and HANS device as the rescue workers peered inside. Dropping the window net, she carefully got out.

As she stepped dizzily down to the pavement, she looked around for Kyle Jordan's car. She found it, crumpled against the outside wall. *Oh, man.* He was going to be pissed at her.

Thirty minutes later, they released her from the infield care center. A throng of reporters was waiting for her, and as soon as she stepped outside, someone shoved a microphone into her face.

"Shelly, Kyle Jordan says you intentionally took him out. How do you answer that?"

Shelly felt her jaw tighten. With a concerted effort, she forced herself to stay cool, to speak calmly. "I haven't had a chance to see the replay yet, but I was just trying to get around him and he wasn't giving me much room."

"He says you got him loose and spun him out of the way."

Shelly took a swig of lukewarm water before she answered. "Like I said, I haven't seen the replay yet. But everyone's out there to win, you know? The ZippiPrint car was awesome today, and I think we could have won if we'd just gotten back into clean air. I hate to see the day end this way after all the hard work my team put in this weekend."

Mercifully, Pam stepped in then and tugged her toward a waiting golf cart. "You okay?" her PR rep asked her as they sped off.

Shelly nodded. "I'll live."

She tried not to groan aloud as they bounced over the pavement, winding their way through the milling crowd. Every inch of her hurt, and it would be worse in the morning.

When they reached her garage stall, she stifled a curse. Kyle Jordan was there waiting for her. He did *not* look happy.

"What are you, crazy?" he shouted as she stepped down from the cart. "You want to win that badly?"

"It was an accident and you know it. You were loose, Jordan. You should have given me room to pass."

"So you just decided to move me out of the way? How'd that work out for you?" he taunted, his face an ugly, mottled red.

Al stepped between them, holding up one hand. "Easy, Jordan. She says it was an accident."

"Yeah, and I'm getting tired of everyone going easy on her because she's a girl. If she's going to intentionally wreck me, then she's going to answer to me for it like anyone else."

Anger flooding her veins, Shelly stepped up, pointing one finger accusingly at Jordan's chest. "Listen here, you little snot-nosed brat. No one's given me a free pass, I've worked my butt off to get where I am, and I'm getting tired of your mouth. So you better shut it or—"

"Or what?" he interrupted, his pale blue eyes blazing. "What are you going to do, little girl?"

"Enough, Jordan." Al was angry now, the veins in his temple standing out in stark relief. "You better get out of here before I shut you up myself."

The air was tense, electric even. Shelly stood her ground, her hands balled into fists by her sides. Finally, Jordan stepped off. Without another word, he stormed away.

Shelly let out her breath in a rush. "Idiot," she muttered. But the seed of doubt was planted in her mind, nagging at her conscience. *Had* she been too aggressive? She had been so focused on winning, so intent on showing Damon that she was the better driver. Had she let that cloud her judgment?

She would watch the replay, and then decide. If she was wrong…well, then, she would own up to her mistake. That's what she did, after all. She wasn't a jerk like Jordan was, and she wasn't about to ruin her reputation as a clean driver just for the sake of pride.

A half hour later, she knocked on the door to Jordan's team hauler. "Got a sec?" she asked when he opened the door and glared down at her.

Leaving the door ajar, he stepped down to the pavement beside her. "So, did you have a chance to watch that replay yet?" he asked, his voice clipped and cold.

Shelly took a deep, fortifying breath, dreading what she was about to say, but knowing it was the right thing to do. "I did watch it. And you're right. I was impatient and reckless, and I took you out. I owe you an apology."

"Damn straight you do," he grumbled, readjusting the cap on his head.

Ugh, of all the people to have to apologize to. Jordan's ego was the size of Texas, and he wasn't going to make this any easier.

"I'd, uh…I'd like to apologize to John, too." Jordan's team owner. "Is he around?"

"You just missed him."

"I'll give him a call later, then. I really *am* sorry." She shook her head. "I was just so focused on winning today. It's no excuse, but when I'm wrong, I admit I'm wrong."

"Yeah, well, payback's a bitch."

Shelly sucked in her breath. "You wouldn't dare!"

"Hey," he said with a shrug, "I just race to win, baby."

She wanted to hit him. Hit him and spit on him. She wouldn't, of course, but it took every ounce of restraint to clamp her mouth shut and keep her hands by her sides.

No way would she sink to his level. Too bad his legions of fans weren't around to see the real Kyle Jordan in action. The media loved to call him a "class act." Class act my—

"Are you finished groveling?" he asked, glancing back over his shoulder toward the hauler behind him. "I was right in the middle of some important business."

Discussing the sponsorship deal with Damon, no doubt.

She nodded. "Sure. Anyway, I apologize. I hope you'll be smart enough to let it go at that."

"Yeah, whatever." Like a sullen child, he stomped back inside the hauler, slamming the door behind him.

DAMON BARELY HAD TIME to force the grin off his face as he stepped back into the hauler's conference room. He'd stood just inside the open doorway during Jordan's entire exchange with Shelly, listening to every word they'd said.

What a woman. His blood raced through his veins, warming his skin. It took every ounce of restraint he possessed to keep from chasing after her, from taking her in his arms and kissing that sweet mouth of hers again. After all, he'd thought of nothing else for nearly a week now. Over and over again, he'd replayed that kiss in his mind, remembering the way her body had pressed against his, making every single nerve ending come alive.

She was truly something special—there was no denying it. And not because he wanted her more than he'd ever wanted any other woman. It was so much more than that. It took guts to admit you were wrong, especially to someone like Kyle Jordan, who wouldn't give an inch. Damon was sure that Jordan wouldn't have apologized to Shelly, had the situation been reversed.

He was equally certain that Shelly would never consider purposely wrecking another driver for the sake of revenge. His estimation of Kyle Jordan had plummeted as his respect for Shelly had skyrocketed. Her integrity spoke volumes about her character.

Maybe he'd underestimated her. Maybe she was far better suited to the sponsorship than he'd originally believed. After all, character and integrity were vital to Pebble Valley Winery. They indicated quality. A brand one could trust. And who personified that better than someone like Shelly Green, no matter how rough around the edges she might be?

Could he set his personal feelings aside and make a business decision?

Kyle Jordan came off as well-spoken and intelligent. He said all the right things in interviews, always slick and polished. And even more importantly, he knew the difference between a Merlot and a Cabernet, could easily discuss the advantages of California wines over, say, their New Zealand counterparts. For all Damon knew, he had studied up in anticipation of their meeting. If that were the case, it demonstrated that he was a quick learner.

But it was all a facade, he realized. There was no substance behind any of it. It was a role that Kyle Jordan played for the cameras, for his sponsors, for his fans. Shadowing the man for three days had made that crystal-clear.

But Shelly…Shelly was the genuine article. The real McCoy. If she believed it, she said it. And if she said it, she meant it. It had only taken him a few days in *her* company to figure that out.

"You'll have to excuse me," he said, moving toward the door just as Jordan strode back inside. "I've got a call to make. But we'll be in touch."

He left Jordan standing there openmouthed, a look

of surprise on his face. Fifteen minutes and a phone call to Steve Clayton later, Damon stepped up to Shelly's motor home and rapped on the door.

Her little dog started yapping away, and he could hear Shelly inside, shushing it, probably putting it back in the bedroom before she answered the door.

Finally, the door swung open. "I told you to give me fifteen min—oh, you're not Al."

"Ah, no." Rocking back on his heels, he shoved his hands into his pockets. "Sorry about that."

She looked somewhat flustered. "No, it's okay. I was just…I mean, we were going to go get something to eat."

"I'll only take a minute of your time."

"Do you want to come inside?" She stepped aside, opening the door wide.

"Sure, just for a minute." He'd make it brief. Probably didn't look good for him to be holing up inside her motor home, now that he thought about it. Then again, this was business. The fact that she was a woman was immaterial, really. Or, at least, it should be.

Who am I kidding? He could deny it all he wanted, but there was no way he could think of Shelly as anything *but* a woman. He stepped inside, forcing himself to ignore the fact that her damp hair smelled of coconut again—vanilla, too. Such sweet, innocent scents, and yet there was something undeniably sexy about Shelly, too. She was full of contradictions. Maybe that was what made her so intriguing?

Or maybe it was the fact that she was so wholly natural, so completely unaware of her feminine power.

Her hair fell to her shoulders in soft waves, pulled off her face with a simple headband. She wore little makeup—maybe some gloss on her lips, but that was the extent of it. And her simple black tank top and narrow, clingy jeans spoke of comfort, not fashion.

He allowed his gaze to sweep appreciatively from her head to her feet, thinking what a crime it was to hide those curves beneath a shapeless racing uniform. And then he realized that she was speaking to him.

"...some iced tea, or something?" she was saying, and he shook his head to clear it.

"No, thanks. I… Uh, are you okay after that hard hit today? I was listening to the scanner. It sounded awful."

"Yeah, I just had the wind knocked out of me for a minute there. Trust me, I've taken harder hits than that and lived to tell the tale."

"But you're okay?" he pressed. Truth was, he'd been scared to death during that moment of silence on her radio. The idea of something happening to her, of losing her…he felt sick even now, just thinking about it.

"Sure." Shelly shrugged dismissively. "They would have sent me to the hospital if I wasn't. It's nothing a little ibuprofen won't cure. Is that what you came to talk to me about?"

"Actually, no. I wanted to relay a message from Steve Clayton. He wants you to come to the winery in Sonoma next week. Monday, after the race in St. Louis if you can, and stay for a couple of days so he can get to know you a little better. I'll be there, too," he added. "I think it's safe to say at this point that you're on our short list for the sponsorship. I'm really impressed by what I've seen so far, and it's time to move on to phase two."

"Phase two?"

"Trying to decide if we're a good fit—on your end as much as ours, actually. It'll give you a chance to sort of interview us, too. See if we're people you're comfortable working with."

"Sounds good to me. Tell Steve that I gratefully accept." Her smile lit up her entire face.

Once again, the urge to kiss her was overwhelming. Damn, but it was impossible not to think about it in her presence. Especially now. After kissing Shelly on the beach in Daytona, there had been no way he could keep pretending that everything was right with Courtney. It had only been a kiss, and yet he'd felt a passion for Shelly that he'd never felt for Courtney, not in all the years they'd been together.

Which was a very bad sign, all things considered. So he'd flown back to New York and officially ended it with Courtney the very next day. It felt like the honorable thing to do, given the circumstances. Mercifully, the breakup had been entirely without dramatics—amicable, even. If anything, Courtney had seemed relieved.

His mother, though…that was a different story. She'd been furious that he'd cheated her out of the perfect daughter-in-law, and what could he say to that? On paper, Courtney *was* perfect.

Just not perfect for him.

In truth, it had been a tough week for him. He'd wanted to call Shelly—in fact, he'd started to several times. But each time, he'd stopped himself. Somehow, he wanted to keep the breakup with Courtney separate from his feelings for Shelly. Then there was the guilt. He'd kissed Shelly *before* he'd ended things with Courtney, and that just wasn't his style. He felt badly about that—and he didn't like feeling badly about something that had felt so right. He didn't want to cast Shelly as the 'other woman.' She deserved better than that.

And so he hadn't called her. Now that he thought about it, it probably hadn't been the right decision. Either way, he felt like an ass.

"Great," he said, forcing his attention back to the beaming woman in front of him, the woman who inexplicably set his blood afire. "I'll arrange for Brent Sanford to fly you out to Sonoma a week from Monday. We'll send a car for you at 8:00 a.m., unless that's too early."

Shelly shook her head. "No, that's fine. And thanks, Damon. I really do appreciate it."

"We appreciate your willingness to fly all the way out there, when you could be home relaxing. Okay, I guess that's it, then."

He had no idea how he was going to keep his feelings for Shelly-the-woman separate from his feelings for Shelly-the-sponsorship candidate. He was going to have to figure out a way to do it, though—somehow. The vineyard trip was business, and he had to keep that at the forefront of his mind. This wasn't about him, after all. It was about Pebble Valley Winery. And to forget that would make him nothing but a selfish bastard. He had to do this *right,* or else he might as well recuse himself from the decision. He would also make sure Steve didn't think he was playing favorites.

There was a loud rap on the door, eliciting more yaps from the dog in the back of the motor home.

"That'll be Al. Do you want to go get some dinner with us?" Shelly asked, almost shyly. "Nothing fancy, we were just going to go grab some burgers."

Keep it business-like, he reminded himself. If he went to eat with her, he'd end up walking her back. And if he walked her back, he'd be tempted to kiss her again, and if he kissed her again, well...

"No, but thanks," he finally said, cutting off the dangerous train of thought. "I've got to get back to New York tonight."

"You're not staying for the race tomorrow?"

"No, I've got some business ends to tie up, and I want to get a jump on it."

The rapping on the door grew more insistent. "Hey, Shel?" came Al's muffled voice. "I'm not getting any younger out here, you know."

"I'd better open up before he has a stroke," Shelly said. "Just hold your horses," she called out, hurrying over to the door.

"It's about time," Al said when the door swung open. Shock registered on his face when he saw Damon standing there. "Oh, I didn't know you had company. I'll come back later."

"No, Damon's just leaving, Al. And get that look off your face, it's not what you think."

"If you say so," Al said with a grin.

Damon turned toward Shelly, suddenly feeling awkward. "I'll see you a week from Monday, then. Al, it's good to see you. Everyone have a safe trip home."

"You, too." Shelly followed him to the door. "And thanks again."

"Hey, don't thank me. You deserve it," he said with a smile.

And he meant it. He only hoped he didn't screw it up.

CHAPTER EIGHT

"Hmm." Becky Peters tapped her chin with one perfectly manicured fingertip. "Let's start with the basics. The dress has got to go. It makes you look twelve years old. You need something way more sophisticated than that. Something business-casual, professional but feminine."

Shelly had put on her second-best dress for today's inspection—a floaty, baby-doll kind of thing. She couldn't wear her best dress, because she'd worn it the last time she'd traveled to Steve Clayton's vineyard. Damon had seen her in it, which meant she had to go to plan B this time around. But judging by the look on Becky's model-perfect face, plan B wasn't going to cut it.

"Okay, new outfit. Anything else?" she muttered.

Becky circled her, her mouth pursed as she continued her examination.

"We have to do something about your hair. Nothing too extreme, because you've got gorgeous hair. Just a little…shaping, maybe."

Shelly nodded. "I have to be able to get it into a ponytail, though."

"That won't be a problem. How do you feel about bangs?"

"Bangs?" The word made her shudder, remembering the slightly uneven, straight-across-her-forehead bangs from her childhood. Her mom's handiwork, of course.

Becky took a lock of Shelly's hair in her fingers and twirled it, drawing it down across her forehead. "Just a little something angled across your eyes. Nothing too major."

"Maybe," Shelly muttered noncommittally.

Becky released the hair and stepped back, peering thoughtfully at Shelly's face. "You don't really need much in the way of makeup. Your skin is beautiful. Maybe just a little something to oomph up your eyes and make them pop. Your eyes are amazing—we should really play them up, make them the focus."

Shelly couldn't help the smile that spread across her face. That was a lot of compliments—and about her looks, no less. "Sounds good," she agreed, liking Becky more by the minute. "Anything else?"

"Hmm, I like the lip gloss, but you could use a bit more color. Something rosier, maybe even a hint of mauve."

Shelly shrugged. "Whatever you say. I totally defer to your expertise."

And Becky *was* an expert—tall and gorgeous, she'd been modeling NASCAR apparel for years, both in print and online. When Shelly had decided she needed a new look before heading out to Sonoma next week, Becky was the first person she'd thought of.

Considering Becky's hectic schedule, Shelly was

grateful that she had agreed to spend the day helping her out. Truth was, she was completely clueless about fashion and beauty products—or anything girlie, for that matter. She needed all the help she could get.

It wasn't that she was opposed to girlie stuff. She loved to get a pedicure, found it relaxing after a busy weekend at the track. And she liked soft, feminine things—thus the floaty baby-doll dress she was wearing, and the sundresses hanging in her closet. She liked to wear her hair long, too, even though short hair would have made her life a lot easier.

It was just that she didn't have a lot of time to indulge in stuff like flipping through fashion magazines or figuring out beauty routines. Growing up, she hadn't had any money for shopping, and now that she had money, she didn't have time. Add to that the fact that she was almost always entirely surrounded by men, and, well…she had no choice but to keep it simple.

With an almost catlike grace that Shelly couldn't help but admire, Becky sauntered to the foyer and reached for her purse on the hall console. "I think that's it. Now it's time to shop, and then pay a visit to my hairdresser. You ready?"

"Ready?" Shelly asked, momentarily confused. She'd thought this was just a consultation of sorts.

She missed hanging out with girlfriends, Shelly realized. Pretty much all of her friends were guys. Not by choice, really, it was just that she didn't have much opportunity to meet women her age. Occasionally she'd go out to eat or to the movies with Holly, the receptionist at Sanford Racing's shop, but that was about the extent of her circle of female friends. Pretty sad, now that she thought about it.

Becky arched one brow, smiling broadly as she hiked her bag onto her shoulder. "What did you think? That I was going to give you advice and then send you out on your own? Come on, it'll be painless. I just hope your credit card is ready for some serious action."

"Sounds fun, but are you sure you're up to this? I hate dragging you out all banged up like that." Shelly frowned, taking in Becky's gauze-wrapped thumb and wrist.

"It's not as bad as it looks, I promise. Anyway, we should get going. Jake's waiting in the car. After Sunday, he won't let me out of his sight. My own personal body-guard," she added with a sigh.

From what Shelly had heard, Becky and Jake McMasters—a private investigator—had surprised an intruder in Jake's office on Sunday when they'd returned from the race in Chicago. Shelly didn't know the details, just that Becky had somehow gotten hurt in the process. Pretty scary stuff, but Becky seemed to be holding up well enough.

"Jake's been sitting out there all this time?" Shelly quickly looked for her purse and keys, then headed toward the door, Becky in tow. "Why didn't you tell me? He could've come in and had a drink or something."

"Nah, he had some phone calls to make. Anyway, he's trying not to be 'obtrusive.'" Becky rolled her eyes as she waited for Shelly to lock the door.

Shelly took a deep breath and headed toward the

waiting car, knowing this was something she needed to do if she wanted the sponsorship. She wanted to look her absolute best when she stepped off that plane in Sonoma—she needed to look just right if she wanted to be the face of Pebble Valley Winery.

This was simply another way of moving her career forward. Gaining polish, sophistication. And it had to be more than superficial—she knew that. The makeover was simply the first step. After all, she wasn't one to back down from a challenge. Everything took effort, and enhancing her own personal image shouldn't be any different. There was more to being a race-car driver than simply driving a race car. As much as she'd resisted that notion in the past—insisting it was all about skill, about talent—she knew it was true. If she wanted to make it in the NASCAR Sprint Cup Series, she needed to step up her game, take it to the next level. It was as simple as that.

Just as she'd struggled to move her career forward in the past, this sponsorship—and any girlie thing she had to do to get it—was simply another way of improving herself and advancing her career.

And there was no point in lying about it, at least, not to herself. She wanted to look her very best, her most appealing, for Damon, too.

All she could do was hope that her best was good enough.

TAKING A DEEP, CALMING breath, Shelly stepped out of the car and onto the gravel drive below. The driver retrieved her bag from the trunk and carried it up to the front porch before driving off in a cloud of dust. The sun was high, the sky a cloudless blue as she turned toward the massive house, shielding her eyes from the sun's glare with one hand.

Carefully, she picked her way across the drive, hoping beyond hope that she didn't twist her ankle in the process. When she finally reached the porch, she simply stood by her bag for a full minute, taking a few deep breaths as she mentally composed herself.

She couldn't help but feel a little silly in her crisp new clothes, her hair perfectly styled and her nails painted a pale shell pink. Okay, maybe *silly* wasn't the right word, but she didn't quite feel like herself.

Despite her unease, she knew she looked great. Thanks to Becky, the miracle worker, her bag was filled with an entirely new wardrobe, classy and chic, and she'd managed to perfect the basic makeup routine that Becky had devised for her. A gentle sweep of eye shadow, the barest touch of mascara and rosy gloss on her lips—that was it. So simple.

And yet she could barely believe how different she looked when she glanced in a mirror. The hairstyle had taken some getting used to, particularly the fringe of bangs that angled over one eye. But she couldn't deny that it was an improvement. She felt feminine and sexy, somehow empowered. It was impossible *not* to feel confident, even if the wedge heels she was wearing did challenge her sense of balance.

I can do this, she told herself. If she could handle a 750-horsepower car, she could certainly handle Steve

Clayton and Damon Tieri and whatever challenges they
hurled her way. Challenges were her specialty, after all.
Hadn't she'd come back from her DNF at Chicago with
a third-place finish in St. Louis, taking the points lead
away from Kyle Jordan?

Damn straight. She was on top right now, and she
planned on staying there. Confidence flowed through
her, like the adrenaline surge she got whenever she
climbed inside a race car. Calmness settled over her, her
race-day focus taking over her mind.

She was ready. With a steady hand, she reached out
and rang the doorbell.

DAMON WATCHED SHELLY over the rim of his wineglass,
still completely blown away by her transformation. It
had taken him a full five minutes to recover when Rosita
had shown Shelly in that afternoon—all he could do was
gape, unable to speak a single word in greeting. Luckily,
Steve had taken over, showing her around the house
and settling her into a guest room before they'd assem-
bled in the living room and got down to business.

By then Damon had found his voice, though he let
Steve lead the discussion. Which was good, because it
left him more time to try and figure out exactly what
Shelly had done to herself since he'd seen her last. She'd
always been beautiful, but now…now she displayed a
confidence and poise he'd never seen her possess when
she wasn't wearing that green-and-purple ZippiPrint
racing uniform. There was something different about
her hair, too, and her eyes.

Before, she'd appeared all innocence. Now, she almost looked sultry. Gone was the girlish sundress she'd worn the last time she'd come to Sonoma. Instead, she was wearing something that looked as though it might have come from Courtney's closet, instead—a tight, fitted khaki skirt that ended just below her knees, paired with a crisp white blouse, a wide black belt cinched at her waist. Very businesslike, and damn if she didn't look sexy as hell.

He set down the wineglass, trying to force his mind back to the business at hand. The sponsorship—Shelly was there to talk about the sponsorship, not for him to ogle her. Even now, she and Steve were animatedly discussing the ways in which wine could be marketed at races, and Shelly had shown a great deal of business savvy with her questions and suggestions. Damon could tell that Steve was impressed by her—his expression said it all.

He wondered if Steve had noticed that Shelly hadn't touched her wine, though. Oh, she'd picked up her glass several times, swirling it around and bringing the glass to her lips. But it remained just as full now as it had been when they'd sat down to dinner nearly two hours ago.

Did it matter? He wasn't quite sure how to answer that one. Maybe. Maybe not. He turned his attention back to Steve, trying to get the gist of the conversation.

"That's why I'm letting Damon make the final decision," Steve was saying. "Without his capital investment, Pebble Valley wouldn't be able to afford a major sponsorship like this. Sure, I know NASCAR and I know wine, but I don't know jack about business. Damon's the expert there."

"You know more than you let on," Damon said, joining the conversation at last.

Shelly turned toward him with a look of surprise on her face, as if she'd just remembered his presence there at the table.

"Not to change the subject," Steve directed at Shelly, "but did you hear the news about the Alan Cargill case? Lucas Haines called Alan's son, Nathan, to tell him that the NYPD has charged some petty street criminal with Cargill's murder."

Shelly nodded. "Yeah, everyone was talking about it in St. Louis this weekend. I heard that Haines isn't convinced they've got the right man, though."

Damon had no idea what they were talking about, but before he had the chance to ask, the phone rang. Several seconds later, Rosita called out for Steve. "It's your lawyer," the woman added, and Steve immediately shoved off from the table.

"If you'll excuse me," he said. "Damon, why don't you take Shelly outside and show her around the grounds? Looks like we're going to get one hell of a sunset tonight."

"Sounds like a good idea." Damon put his napkin on the table and pushed back his chair. "If you're up for it, Shelly. I know it's been a long day."

"I'm fine." Shelly glanced down at her feet, then back up at him, smiling ruefully. "I might have to change out of these shoes if we're going to walk very far, though."

"We won't go far," he promised. He liked those shoes way too much. They made her legs look impossibly long, her calves sculpted and tanned and toned.

With a nod, she rose. "Okay, then. Lead the way."

For a quarter hour they walked around the grounds immediately surrounding the house. He told her a little bit of the winery's history as they strolled, repeating what he'd learned only recently from Steve himself.

Eventually they came to a stone bench in a little arbor that overlooked row after row of grapevines. "Would you like to sit?" Damon asked, pausing. "This is the perfect spot to watch the sunset. It's really something to see."

"Sure," Shelly said, lowering herself to the stone bench. Crossing her legs, she propped an elbow on one knee, gazing out toward the horizon expectantly. "It's really beautiful here, isn't it? I love this part of California."

"So do I," he agreed with a nod.

Shelly glanced up at him, her fair hair falling across one eye. "You seem…right at home here, actually."

Damon took a deep breath, inhaling the warm, scented air. "It feels like home."

"But it's nothing like New York."

"I think maybe I've had enough of New York for a while." He realized it was the truth as soon as the words left his lips, though he'd never before acknowledged it. For the first time in his thirty-five years, he was living his *own* life. Away from the family business, from the constant interference in his life, from the responsibilities that had become his thanks to his brother's failures—failures in their parents' eyes, at least.

By all accounts, Mario was perfectly happy living off his trust fund, in a loft in SoHo with his wife, Tricia. They had no children and no plans to have any. Tricia was a performance artist, and though Damon had never been able to discern what, exactly, made her work "art," it seemed to make her happy.

Maybe Mario was the smart one, after all, Damon realized. Off charting his own course, living his own life rather than the one carefully plotted out for him.

And Shelly was definitely off that course, no doubt about it. His parents would be horrified to learn he was entertaining feelings for her. He could just imagine them ticking off her so-called transgressions—she grew up in Alabama, she didn't go to college, her mother had raised her alone and was likely an alcoholic, to boot. Her family wasn't their kind, they'd say—a euphemism for "not of their class." Before now, that might have meant something to him, too.

But now, sitting beside her, he realized it meant nothing. This was *his* life, not theirs. He'd wasted years following their lead, rather than listening to his own heart, his own instincts, even where women were concerned. What kind of man did that make him?

"You're really lost in thought there, aren't you, Tieri?" Shelly asked with a smile, drawing him from his ruminations.

"Sorry. Look," he said, turning his gaze to the sky just as the deep-orange sun melted against the horizon, painting the sky with wide swaths of pink against a lavender canvas.

Shelly let out her breath in a rush. "Wow."

"Yeah, we don't get sunsets like that in Manhattan."

"I suppose not," Shelly murmured. "Thank you for flying me out here," she said suddenly, turning to face him. "Even if I don't get the sponsorship, I appreciate the confidence you've shown in me. Steve says…well, he says you've spoken very highly of me. I realize you don't think my background is right for Pebble Valley, but you've really put yourself out there for me, and I appreciate that."

He couldn't help himself; he reached for her hand, taking it in his. It was cold, he realized, rubbing it between his palms. "Don't thank me, Shelly. You're here because you've earned it. There're still other things to consider, other drivers to consider," he amended. "But you're here entirely on your own merit." He took a deep breath, hoping to slow the burn that was spreading through his veins.

"I'm trying to do this right, Shelly. Keep it all business. I have to do it that way, can't let my personal feelings get in the way here. I hope you understand that."

Her eyes met his, nearly knocking the breath from his lungs. The light of the moon glanced off her hair, illuminating her eyes, making her skin glow spectacularly. He felt like a sixteen-year-old boy, all raging hormones and rampant lust. It was a good thing that Steve was back at the house, or else he'd be tempted to sweep her up in his arms and carry her back to his bed. Not that she'd let him, but he'd certainly give it the old college try.

"What are you trying to say, Damon?" she asked, confusion written all over her face.

"I don't know," he answered, shaking his head. "I just wish that, for a few minutes, we could forget about the sponsorship altogether. Put it aside and just be two people sitting on a bench, watching the sunset together."

"Actually, you're too late for that. It already set," Shelly said, and Damon couldn't help but laugh.

"So it did."

"We could be watching the stars come out, instead," she offered, a slight catch in her voice.

Was she feeling the same things he was feeling? He couldn't be sure. She'd seemed totally businesslike all day, never giving him any indication that this attraction he felt was reciprocated. In fact, she'd almost gone out of her way to ignore him, to work her charm on Steve, instead. What exactly did that mean? You'd think with three sisters he'd have a better understanding of the workings of the female mind, but he had nothing.

The last thing he wanted was for her to think that his advances were somehow tied to the sponsorship deal. Damon prided himself on his ethics, his personal code of avoiding all gray areas where business standards were concerned. But right now he was walking a thin line, and he knew it. Unfortunately, that didn't make him want her any less.

She shivered then, her hand still clasped in his. "You're cold," he said, frowning. The temperature had dropped markedly since the sun had set.

She shook her head. "No. I'm not, I swear. It's just…"

"Just what?" he pressed.

She shook her head. "Nothing."

"It's going to drive me crazy if you don't tell me what you're thinking," he urged, overwhelmed with curiosity. Shelly was a mystery he wanted to solve—*needed* to solve.

She let out her breath in a rush. "I don't know. Whenever I'm around you, it's just… Never mind, it's too embarrassing." She looked away, suddenly unable to meet his eyes.

Dropping her hand, he reached for her chin, holding it between his thumb and forefinger, forcing her gaze back to his. "You have no idea how badly I want to kiss you," he said, his voice a hoarse whisper.

"Why don't you, then?" she challenged, her voice wavering slightly.

Damon closed his eyes and took a deep, steadying breath. He leaned toward her, nuzzling the side of her neck, feeling her pulse pound beneath his lips. "Nothing to do with the sponsorship, right?" he murmured.

"Right," she said, an urgency in her voice now. Her hands clenched into fists in her lap. "Please, Damon."

She'd called him "Damon," he realized. No more of her jocular "Tieri" nonsense. That was invitation enough. With a low growl, his mouth took hers fiercely, possessively—as if she might change her mind at any minute. Call him selfish, but until she did, he wanted as much of her as he could get.

But she didn't draw away. Instead, she wrapped her hands around his neck, molding herself against him as she opened her mouth against his, his name a sigh on her lips.

All this time he'd thought the winery was paradise, but now…now he knew *this* was, instead.

CHAPTER NINE

"I SEE ROSITA GAVE you my message," Damon said, lowering himself to the picnic blanket beside Shelly, under the shade of a sprawling old oak. "Thanks for agreeing to join me. I thought a picnic might be nice."

"The weather sure is great for it," she said, smiling up at him. "It's a beautiful day, isn't it?" The sky was a perfect blue, not a cloud in sight, and a gentle breeze ruffled the leaves above them.

He glanced up at the sky, squinting. "It is. And I spent the entire morning holed up inside, on a conference call. The time difference between here and New York makes things difficult at times. Anyway, how'd it go this morning? Sorry I missed your tour."

"It was great," Shelly answered, kicking off her shoes and tucking her feet beneath herself. "I can't believe how much Steve knows about winemaking. I mean, I still think of him as a driver, you know? He was always one of my favorites when I was a kid. I kind of had a crush on him," she admitted. With his blond, surfer-boy hair and warm blue eyes, he'd looked like a young Robert Redford. Even now, he was incredibly good-looking. And his multiple championships spoke for his talent.

Damon lifted the towel off the picnic basket and peered inside, frowning. "How many people did Rosita think she was feeding? There's enough food in here for an army."

"Good, because I'm starving," Shelly said, her stomach rumbling in anticipation. Or maybe it was just nerves. Being with Damon did that to her, especially after last night's kiss. She wasn't quite sure where things stood right now, but it seemed best to keep the conversation on business for now. After all, it was what she'd come to Sonoma for.

"Looks like we've got ham, turkey or chicken salad. Wait, there's roast beef, too."

"I'll take chicken salad." Shelly took the sandwich he handed her.

"We've got crudités." He pulled out a plastic container and set it down beside her. "There must be some dip somewhere."

Pulling off the lid, she found a variety of sliced veggies inside—carrots, celery, cucumber, yellow pepper strips.

Shelly leaned over and peeked inside the basket. "I hope Rosita put some ranch dressing in there." Her stomach actually grumbled in anticipation.

He shook his head. "Doesn't look like it, but we've got hummus, instead. And some cheese. Jarlsberg, maybe? Grapes and apples, too."

"You weren't kidding, were you? Did she think Steve was coming with us?"

"Maybe," he said with shrug.

"He said he had some phone calls to make," she said, reaching for a cucumber slice and popping it into her mouth.

Shelly busied herself unwrapping her sandwich while Damon opened a bottle of sparkling water and poured it into two glasses. Real glass, not plastic. They sure knew how to do picnics at Pebble Valley Winery. Of course, she hated sparkling water, but she decided to keep that fact to herself.

"So, what did you study in college? At Princeton, wasn't it?" she asked, deciding that her best bet was to get Damon talking about himself. The more they talked about him, the less they'd talk about her.

"Economics," he said around a bite of sandwich. Roast beef, Shelly noted with satisfaction. Somehow it seemed the manly choice. "Pretty dry."

"The sandwich?"

"No, economics."

"Well, why'd you study it, then?" she asked, then took a bite of her own sandwich. It was delicious, actually. Chicken and apples and walnuts and celery. Plus something else she couldn't identify. She'd have to ask Rosita for the recipe. She could give it to Charlie—he loved chicken salad, too.

"Actually, I'm not sure why. It just made business sense, I guess. My father had studied economics, so it seemed like the logical choice."

"Well, what would you have liked to study instead?"

He appeared to ponder the question while he chewed

his sandwich. "Maybe art history. Yeah, I think I would have liked that."

She almost choked on her food. "Really? Art history? I have to admit, I can't really see that. You don't look the type."

He shrugged, reaching for a carrot stick. His sleeve was rolled up to his elbow, and Shelly couldn't help but admire his exposed forearm. His skin was tanned and muscular, dusted with dark hair. There was something very masculine about Damon, something that appealed to her on some weird, primal level.

"I like fine art," he said with a shrug. "I could walk around the Louvre for days on end."

"Ahh, Paris. I've never been there."

For a moment, he looked confused. "Never been to the Louvre, or never been to Paris?"

"Neither," she answered with a shrug.

His brows came together in obvious disbelief.

"I've never been out of the good ol' U.S. of A., except for races. Mexico City, Montreal. That's it. Hey, will you hand me the hummus?" She'd have to make do, since there wasn't any ranch dressing. She didn't much like hummus.

"Sure, here you go." He handed her a round plastic container.

Shelly took off the lid and wrinkled her nose, then dipped her carrot stick in and took a bite. "Ugh, this stuff is awful. Tastes like dirty feet."

"You know what dirty feet taste like?" Damon asked with a laugh.

"Okay, you got me there. Still, how can you eat this stuff?"

"I kind of like it. Anyway, I can't believe you've never been to Paris. You really should do something about that."

"Maybe someday I will," she said, feeling a bit defensive. "There wasn't money for trips to Europe when I was a kid, and now I'm just so busy, traveling most of the year. Once the season's done, all I want to do is hole up at home and try and live like a normal person for a couple of months."

He nodded. "I guess that makes sense. You said you have a house in Mooresville, right?"

"Yeah, nothing too fancy. It's not on the lake or anything. It didn't make sense to spend a lot of money on a house that I almost never see. But I do have a great custom garage there."

"I'll bet you do. Though Al says you spend a lot of time at the shop."

"I'm interested in what goes on at the shop. To me, racing is more than just hopping in a car on race day. I like to understand my equipment, to help make decisions about it with my team. I know Al likes to make it sound as if I don't have a life—"

"I think he worries about you, that's all."

"Can we change the subject?" she asked, suddenly uncomfortable. "Maybe you could slice off some of that cheese for me."

"Sure," he said, digging around the basket and producing the wedge. "What does Steve have planned for you this afternoon? Did he say?"

Shelly tried not to wince as she took a sip of the sparkling water. "I think he said he's taking me to the tasting room."

"Oh, good." He sliced off a piece of cheese and handed it to her. "Maybe I'll come with you, if you don't mind."

"Sure, why not?"

"So, what do you think of Pebble Valley so far?" he asked, gesturing toward the rows of vines that spread out below them.

"I think it's great. I'm really impressed with what Steve's done here. I never would have imagined it, but it seems like he fits in here just as well as he does at the track."

Damon nodded, as if he approved of her answer. "And how would you feel about working with us?"

"I think I'm pretty comfortable with you both," she hedged. She couldn't quite say what she really felt— that she enjoyed his company, that he made her laugh, that he made her want to refine her rough edges and realize her true potential. Nah, that sounded way too corny. Too…*needy.*

"I mean, you do get on my nerves sometimes, but I guess I could put up with you," she quipped instead, deciding to play it cool.

His mouth widened into a smile. "I'm glad you're back."

"I'm back?" She shook her head, confused.

"Well, it's just that you've been acting so proper and professional, I was worried that you'd left the real Shelly Green at home. I have to admit, I really like her. The one with the sharp-edged tongue, I mean."

She stared at him wide-eyed for a moment, then burst out laughing. "So, we're done with all the interview stuff now?"

"Yeah, we're done. I'm impressed with your restraint, though. You're—" he shook his head "—I don't know, different somehow than when we first met. Here at the winery," he clarified, as if she'd forgotten.

She rolled her eyes. "I definitely came on a little strong that day. I wasn't quite ready for what I was asking for, not yet. But you must admit, you acted like a jerk."

"You're right. I did, and I'm sorry for it." He looked truly repentant. "You're not the only one who's changed since that day."

"I really want this sponsorship, Damon," she said, all seriousness now.

He reached for her hand, stroking the back of it with his thumb. "I know you do, Shelly. Just…be yourself, okay?"

"I can do that," she said with a nod. In fact, she much preferred it. She glanced down at her hand, still clasped in his, and smiled. "Were you planning on flirting with all of your candidates?"

"Nah, only the pretty ones," he answered with a grin.

"I guess that rules out Kyle Jordan, then."

He grimaced. "Well, you never know. I guess if you put a dress on him—"

"Yuck!" Shelly exclaimed in mock horror. "Don't even go there. I just ate, you know."

Favoring her with his movie-star smile, he stood

and reached for her hand. "C'mon, if you're done, let's go. The tasting room awaits."

SHELLY AWOKE WITH A start. It took her several seconds to get her bearings, to realize she was in a strange bed, a strange house. The vineyard, she told herself groggily. In Sonoma.

There was a commotion downstairs. She could hear the housekeeper's voice, and then another loud voice that sounded oddly familiar, and yet totally out of place. A deep baritone joined in, one she recognized as Steve Clayton's. She could've sworn she'd heard her name.

What the heck was going on? Jumping out of bed, she hurried to her small suitcase and rifled through it, looking for something she could throw on quickly and easily. Of course, all she'd packed was nice things—not a single pair of easy-to-get-on sweats. Jeans would have to do, she realized, finding the one pair she'd decided to throw in, just in case she found herself overdressed in the skirts and tailored trousers Becky had made her buy.

She struggled into the jeans, then pulled her nightshirt over her head and tossed it to the ground.

A button-up blouse would have to do—she didn't have anything more casual than that.

The voices downstairs grew louder as Shelly shoved her arms into her shirt's sleeves and hurried to fasten the buttons, her fingers clumsy and awkward. Quickly, she ran a brush through her hair, roughly pulling at the snags and pushing her bangs into place.

Only as she opened her room's door and stepped out

into the hall did she remember that she hadn't brushed her teeth, but the all-too-familiar voice she heard at the bottom of the steps made it impossible to turn back now.

"Look, are you going to go up there and get my daughter, or aren't ya?" her mother slurred, sounding drunk.

No.

Panic made her heart race, her stomach lurch. For a moment, she froze. Then she stumbled down the stairs, nearly tripping over her own feet in her rush.

"Ma, what are you doing here?"

Everyone turned to stare at her, there on the landing. Steve, Damon, even Rosita, the housekeeper.

"Well, it's about time," her mother called out accusingly. Missy stumbled, and Steve reached for her elbow to steady her. "They towed away my car, Shelly! Just showed up and drove away with it. I only missed two payments, just two."

Shelly swallowed hard, attempting to find her voice. "And you came all the way out here to California to tell me this? It couldn't wait a few days?"

"No, it couldn't wait a few days. Didn't you hear what I said? They took my car! You've got to do something about it. I tried to call, but your cell phone kept going straight to voice mail."

How on earth had her mother missed two payments? Shelly sent her money every month, enough to cover the mortgage and car payment, plus some. Up till now, Missy had made every payment, on time. And her stupid cell phone—she'd forgotten to charge it before she left

North Carolina. She'd only realized it was dead when she'd reached the winery, but figured it didn't matter much. The shop knew where to find her. But her mother?

"How did you know where I was?" she asked, trying her best to keep her voice steady.

"That nice woman at your shop, the one who has manners. Holly, or Molly somethin' or other. Told me you came here, and I figured it wasn't right, you getting a fancy vacation while I'm stuck at home with no car. How am I supposed to get to work?"

"This isn't a vacation, Ma. I'm here on business." Shelly shook her head, ignoring her mother's snort. "How did you even get here?"

"I grew wings and flew. How ya think I got here? I used that credit card you gave me, the one for emergencies. Figured this was emergency enough. Got in after midnight last night. Had to stay in an ol' fleabag motel out by the airport till I could get a cab here this morning. Least they had a bar."

Shelly covered her face with her hands. This couldn't be happening. It was a bad dream, a very bad dream. But when she dropped her hands, her mother was still there, Steve Clayton holding her steady as she swayed on her feet, her mascara smeared beneath her eyes, her blood-red lipstick looking garish.

Her humiliation was complete.

"I'll call them, Ma," Shelly said at last. "Just give me a few minutes, and I'll see what I can do, okay?"

"In the meantime, how about some coffee?" Steve offered, and Shelly felt tears sting her eyes.

How could Missy do this to her? Of all the selfish, irresponsible things Missy had done, this was pretty much the worst. Absolute rock-bottom. She glanced over at Damon and saw the pity etched on his face— pity and something else, something she couldn't quite identify. Probably disgust, she realized.

Missy allowed Steve to lead her away, toward the kitchen, Rosita following behind, wringing her hands. That left her and Damon alone, and Shelly felt bile rise in her throat, remembering the kiss they'd shared the night before last, imagining how he must feel about that now.

"If you'll excuse me for a minute," she managed to choke out, then turned and fled up the stairs as fast as she could go. She barely made it to the bathroom before she began to retch, her stomach emptying itself of its contents.

Ten minutes later, she'd managed to wash her face and brush her teeth. It was time to go back downstairs and face the music. What else could she do?

When she reached the bottom of the stairs, Damon was there waiting for her. "Steve's working his charm on her in the kitchen, plying her with coffee, and then he's going to get Rosita to settle her into a guest room for a while. Let her sleep it off."

Shelly swallowed hard, unable to meet his eyes. "Thanks," she murmured. "I'll…uh, I'll get her on a flight tonight. I'll just go pack up my things."

"No, we'll take care of getting her home. You look like you could use some fresh air. Maybe we can rustle up some breakfast out on the patio."

Shelly shook her head. "I don't think I could eat

anything." Just the thought of food made her stomach pitch.

"Okay, then a walk?"

"Damon, you don't have to—"

"I want to," he interrupted, reaching for her hand.

Tears burned behind her eyes, threatening to spill over. "I'm *so* sorry about this."

"C'mon," Damon urged, tugging on her hand. "Let's get outside, and then we'll talk."

Shelly just nodded and allowed him to lead her out.

Minutes later, she found herself sitting on the same stone bench as before, gazing out on the vineyard's grounds, a warm palette of greens and golds, the air scented with grapes. So peaceful, and yet inside she was anything but.

This was nothing short of a disaster, and just when everything was going so well, too. After yesterday's picnic, Steve had spent the afternoon with her in the tasting room, explaining the subtleties of the different varieties of his wines. Damon had joined them, and she had to admit, it had been both interesting and educational.

Dinner had been enjoyable, even though it was obvious that Damon was trying to keep his distance. And she couldn't blame him, not really. It was hard to keep business and pleasure separate in a situation like this—she wasn't quite sure how to handle it, herself. So they'd both backed down from what seemed to be a mutual attraction, though she could barely credit the notion that he was as into her as she was to him.

Still, last night had ended on a high note. Steve had indicated that Shelly had his full approval; the ball was now in Damon's court. And then *this* had to go and happen.

"You want to talk about it?" Damon asked, his voice soft, almost comforting.

Despite the sun's warmth, a shiver worked its way down her spine. "I don't even know what to say."

"Are you okay?" He reached for her hand and took it in his, giving it a little squeeze.

She returned the pressure. "Yeah, I'm fine. But I can't imagine what you must be thinking right now."

"Just that I've been in similar situations before, courtesy of my brother. I know how difficult it is. But you can't control other people, no matter how hard you try."

Shelly exhaled slowly before speaking. "I know, but that doesn't make it any easier. Or any less embarrassing."

"Once, when I'd just graduated from business school and launched my first fund, I had a meeting with some of my investors. My brother showed up at my office, and let's just say he wasn't feeling any pain. I'm lucky none of the investors bailed on me. After that, my father banned him from the offices. Permanently. Mario was so angry, he didn't speak to me for months."

"Was he… I mean, did he make a habit out of showing up in places like that?"

"Nah, not really. Mario just likes to have fun. I think he'd planned on finding me holed up at the office, working late, and he thought he was doing me a favor. His intentions were good enough. He just doesn't think things through, that's all."

"Nothing like his brother, huh?"

"Mario and I are about as different as night and day," Damon agreed with a nod, smiling crookedly.

"Are you two close at all?"

Damon brushed a speck of lint from his khakis. "Not really. Mostly my fault, though. I always blamed him for running out on the family, for refusing to do anything he was supposed to do. Because that meant it all fell to me, instead. Everything I've done in my life, I've done to please my family. I went to Princeton because my father did. Majored in economics even though I hated it. Went to business school afterward because it was expected of me. Took over the family business, because who else was going to do it? My father was getting old, and my mother wanted to travel. Mario was off living it up in Europe at the time and Kate was ready to start a family…" He trailed off, shaking his head.

"But you're so good at what you do," Shelly protested. Hadn't she read that he was some sort of Wall Street whiz kid? That his hedge fund—and yes, she'd looked up *hedge funds,* so now she had a better understanding of how they worked—had earned record profits? That he'd been a multimillionaire by the time he was thirty?

Damon just shrugged. "I enjoy a challenge. And for a while, managing the fund was challenging. That doesn't mean I would have chosen that particular career path, given the choice. Though who knows, maybe I would have. I'm pretty sure I wouldn't have felt the same pressure, though, had I come to it on my own."

Shelly nodded, though the concept of parental pressure was entirely foreign to her.

"Anyway," he continued, "no family is perfect. We all have our challenges. We just have to do the best with what we're given."

"Yeah, well, I've had about enough of my challenges," Shelly muttered, her attention now drawn back to her current plight.

Damon cleared his throat uncomfortably. "Has your mother always been this way?" he asked, giving her hand another squeeze.

"You mean a drunk? Yeah, pretty much always. She was always good about keeping it in check, though. You know, only drinking on her days off and never using the rent money or grocery money or anything like that. Not that that made it any easier." Shelly gazed off toward the horizon, to the exact same spot where she'd watched the sun set the night before last.

She'd thought she had the sponsorship in her pocket then, and now…well, now she might as well forget it. Might as well get it all out in the open, all the horrible stuff from her childhood. "It was bad enough growing up poor with no father. We lived in small-town Alabama, after all. The Bible Belt. I didn't have a lot of friends. Still, my mom did her best. She worked two jobs just to make ends meet. How could I blame her if she needed a few drinks now and then to relax?

"She'd pass out on the couch afterward, and I'd just fend for myself till she slept it off. No big deal, really, except I couldn't ever invite anyone over, just in case. I think I first got involved in racing just to get out of the house, you know? Away from her."

"I can imagine," Damon said with a nod. "Did you get any support at all from her?"

"Not really. I mean, she didn't mind my doing it, she just wasn't in any position to help me out, financially. So I worked at a nearby stable to earn extra money, which also got me out of the house. At first I kept the money I made in an envelope hidden in my dresser drawer, but she found it and treated herself to a weekend-long drinking binge once. After that, I opened my own bank account."

"Sounds like a lot of responsibility for a kid. Didn't you have any family who could help you out?"

"No, not really. Just Granny, but she was pretty dependent on us. She passed away the year I graduated from high school. There was an aunt in Atlanta, too, but she and my mom never got along. Really, it wasn't as bad as it sounds," she said, glancing up at him, gauging his reaction. "Like I said, I spent a lot of time at the track."

"That sounds pretty lonely, though," he said. "Especially for a teenager."

Shelly shook her head. "I knew everyone at the track—they were like family. And the couple who owned the stable, they were my first sponsors. They gave me tons of support, let me work around my racing schedule."

"Did you date at all? You know, normal teenage hormones and all that?"

"Nah, the guys I hung out with at the track didn't really think of me as a girl. Besides, I was better than all of them—a better mechanic, a better driver. I beat them all, took every local title. I'm sure that bruised their delicate male egos."

"I'm sure it did," he said with an easy laugh. "You must have been something, though." A force of nature, wasn't that what her crew chief had called her?

"Well, I've never had anyone to depend on but myself," she answered with a shrug. "Looks like some things never change."

"You're not responsible for your mother."

Shelly sighed, looking back over her shoulder toward the house. "I still can't believe she had the nerve to show up here like she did. Steve must be freaking out right now."

"It looked like he had everything under control. Between him and Rosita, I'm sure Missy's being well cared for."

"More than she deserves," Shelly muttered, her anger rising again. Missy had probably single-handedly blown the sponsorship for her, and she didn't even have a clue what she'd done. Probably wouldn't care, either. She only cared about herself. "I guess I should go in and check on her. Make sure she isn't causing any more mayhem."

"I'll go with you," he said, rising and helping her to her feet.

Shelly swallowed a lump in her throat. "Thank you, Damon. For being so understanding, I mean. Anyone ever tell you that you're a good listener?"

"I'm pretty sure they haven't. But hey, I'll take that as a compliment."

She nodded, chewing on her lower lip to keep from saying more. Like how comfortable it felt in his presence, how good it felt to open up to him, how much she wished he would take her in his arms.

As if he'd read her mind, he drew her closer then, wrapping his arms around her and pulling her head to his chest. She couldn't be sure, but she thought she felt his lips in her hair, just above her ear.

How long they stood like that, she couldn't say. She didn't want to move, didn't want to leave his embrace. Inhaling sharply, she breathed in his now-familiar scent, listening to his heart pound in rhythm with her own.

A bird called in the distance, a plaintive cry answered by another. Bees buzzed around them. A car rumbled by. Time passed, and yet it stood still.

When he released her at last, Shelly felt entirely calm, almost serene. "You ready?" he asked, favoring her with his movie-star smile.

"As ready as I'll ever be," Shelly answered with a nod. Whatever happened from here on out, she had gained a friend. A good friend. Someone who listened, who cared.

And maybe—just maybe—that was worth more than a sponsorship.

CHAPTER TEN

SHELLY SET THE WRENCH back in the toolbox, then used the hem of her T-shirt to wipe the sweat from her brow. A smile of self-satisfaction spread across her face as she tossed her filthy coveralls into a bin, mentally cataloging the morning's accomplishments.

She'd managed to change out the GT's starter, check the oil level in the differential, change a water hose and tighten up the oil-pan bolts, all in a couple of hours. Not bad.

She still had a few more things to do, so the car remained up on jackstands. Her state-of-the-art garage was equipped with two hydraulic lifts, but she almost never used them. Call her old-school, but she preferred to lie on her back on a piece of cardboard, right there on the hard concrete floor beneath the cherry-red car.

She checked her watch—one-thirty, which meant she'd succeeded in avoiding her mother's calls all morning. Every time her cell had rung, she'd let it go straight to voice mail, where Missy had no doubt left a half-dozen messages by now.

A prickle of guilt niggled her conscience, but she managed to push it away. Two weeks had passed since that debacle in Sonoma, since she'd called the lending company and straightened things out with Missy's car. Afraid it might happen again, Shelly had actually paid the damn thing off.

But had her mother called to thank her? No, of course not. She hadn't even acknowledged Shelly's generosity, hadn't bothered to apologize or even explain herself.

And now Missy had decided to break her silence, calling off the hook like some rabid telemarketer. Well, right now Shelly didn't feel like speaking to her; she wasn't even sure she could be civil, much less understanding. That little stunt Missy had pulled had seriously messed with Shelly's head.

Al had suggested she make an appointment with a sports psychologist, but she'd brushed aside his offers to set something up. She didn't need a shrink. All she needed was some old-fashioned blood and sweat. Nothing better than lying under a car, your knuckles scraped and bleeding, the smell of oil and steel surrounding you, to get your head back on straight.

As for Damon…well, it turns out she'd found his tender side more of a turn-on than his kisses, if that was at all possible. She'd thought something had happened there between them, something real, something meaningful. But clearly she'd been mistaken. All that talk about keeping his personal feelings separate from the business at hand—apparently that was just lip service.

Instead of being the friend she'd imagined he'd become after their heartfelt talk at the winery, he'd put an emotional distance between them, instead.

Oh, he'd called her—twice, actually. But both calls had been awkward, as if neither was quite sure what to say to the other. The truth was, she wasn't exactly sure what she'd expected from him, except maybe some indication that his feelings for her—whatever they were, exactly—hadn't changed.

It went without saying that he hadn't mentioned the sponsorship. She could only assume that, despite what had seemed like genuine understanding on his part, her mother's appearance there at the vineyard had pretty much ended her bid.

And the truth was, she couldn't really blame him for that. Her mother was a loose cannon—unpredictable, erratic. Until she got Missy under control, she couldn't really consider herself a viable candidate for any big sponsor. Who'd want to take the risk of public embarrassment? She wouldn't, in Damon's place.

And if that wasn't bad enough, the past two races hadn't gone well for her, either. A blown engine had led to a DNF in St. Louis, a track where she usually finished well. And instead of bouncing back the following week in Indianapolis, she'd finished outside the top twenty. Despite a good qualifying run, she'd never gotten into the groove on race day.

She headed over to the sink in the corner to wash up, trying to figure out just what had gone wrong as she squirted a generous amount of soap into her hands and turned on the hot water. Her car had been good, she thought, rubbing her hands together under the near-scalding water, then turning off the tap and drying her hands on an old, stained towel. Not a winning car, but a top-ten car. Maybe even top-five. Maybe she'd been holding back, less aggressive than usual? Or maybe she just wasn't focused enough. Maybe she'd let herself get distracted by her quest for a NASCAR Sprint Cup Series ride.

Way too many maybes.

Whatever the case, she'd lost her points lead. Now she just had to figure out how to get it back. Shaking her head in frustration, she headed inside the house just as her cell phone began to ring. *Again.*

Just great. Total silence for two weeks, and now Missy wasn't going to give her any peace until she answered the damn phone and listened to whatever it was she wanted to say to her.

Might as well get it over with.

"Hey, Ma," she said, lifting the tiny phone to her ear as she sat down on the sofa and kicked her shoes off.

"Where've you been all day? I've been trying to get ahold of you for hours." Just like Missy to go straight to the accusations.

"I was under a car. Sorry. What's up?" Trixie jumped into Shelly's lap, nudging her arm with her damp nose.

"Well, I, uh—" Missy cleared her throat loudly "—I wanted to tell you how sorry I am. For the whole California thing, you know."

"Yeah, I know." Shelly paused, frowning as she

stroked Trixie's soft, downy fur. "You put me in a pretty bad spot. Probably lost me a sponsorship deal."

"I also wanted to let you know that, well, I'm doing something about it now. The drinking," Missy clarified. "I joined a program. You know, one of those twelve-step things."

"Really?" Shelly could barely conceal her surprise. Her mother had never before admitted she had a problem, no matter how bad things had gotten. This was definitely a first.

"I realized when I got home…well, that it was getting worse, that I'd finally hit rock bottom. I've never spent the car money before, never let it get out of hand like that."

"I know you haven't, Ma."

"Anyway, I just wanted you to know. Oh, and I sent a card to Steve Clayton. Apologizing and thanking him for taking such good care of me."

"I'm sure he appreciates it. He's a good guy."

"He sure is. I feel so bad, embarrassing you like that in front of your friends." Her mother's voice broke, and Shelly's hardened heart softened a fraction.

"I'm just glad you're getting some help. If there's anything I can do, anything at all—"

"You've done plenty, Shelly. More'n anyone could expect, really. So…um, where you headed out to this weekend?"

"Iowa, believe it or not. But next week's Watkins Glen. You know, in upstate New York," she added.

"Oh, yeah? You love those road courses, don't you? I'll try and take the day off so I can watch you on TV."

That was the closest to supportive Missy had sounded in a good long time, Shelly realized with a start. Maybe she *was* turning over a new leaf. "Sounds good, Ma. I'll try and win it, then, so I can wave to you from Victory Lane."

Missy laughed. "I just bet you will, too. Well, I've got to run, but I'm glad I caught you. I think I can cross one of them twelve steps off my list now."

"Just take it slowly, Ma. One day at a time, okay?"

"Love you, sweetie."

Shelly felt tears well in her eyes. "I love you, too."

The line went dead, and Shelly just stared at the phone, wondering if she'd imagined the call. It was all just too…unbelievable. Too good to be true. Which probably meant that it was.

Trixie whined, and Shelly scratched her under the chin. "Yeah, I know how you feel. C'mon, let's go for a walk."

"HOW'S IT GOING, Al?" Shelly called out, striding into the shop. "Did we get the new engines in?"

Al stuffed a rag into his back pocket. "Sure did. Seem pretty good, too. I think we'll take one of them to the Glen. I thought you were taking the day off today, going to a movie or something with Holly."

"Yeah, I was. I don't know, I was feeling too restless to sit through a movie. Thought I'd come poke around here a bit instead, look at the latest wind-tunnel data."

Al's eyes narrowed as he studied her face. "Something's eating at you, isn't it? It's this whole sponsorship thing, I bet."

Shelly sighed heavily. "I can't help it, Al. I was so close. I want to blame Missy, but there's no guarantee they'd have given it to me anyway."

"Well, if this one doesn't work out, another one will. I know Adam's working hard, looking for another sponsor. He wants you in the premier series."

"I know." She reached for the clipboard behind Al, listlessly scanning the notes from the last race.

"Then why so glum?" Al asked. "C'mon, fess up. I can read you like a book, you know. It's got something to do with Tieri, something more than the sponsorship. Just what's going on between you two?"

Shelly tried to hide the surprise on her face. "There's nothing going on between us."

"Uh-huh. And I'm the Queen of England. I'm not blind, Shelly. I've seen the way he looks at you, and I've seen the way you look at him, when you think no one's looking. I didn't think he was your type, though. Kind of arrogant, don't you think? A little too slick, too glib."

Shelly shook her head, frustrated. "I don't know what my type is anymore."

"So I'm right? There *is* something going on? I knew it."

"I like him, okay? Let's leave it at that. I feel stupid enough about it as it is—I don't need you teasing me about it. I realize he's completely out of my league."

"Well, you're not a nun, you know. You should stop living like one. Maybe you just need to get out more. Maybe Becky Peters could set you up with someone. How long has it been since you went out on a date? A *real* date?"

"I don't know, since Don," she answered. Al's nephew. "Last year, I guess."

"Since you broke that poor boy's heart," Al said, shaking his head with a scowl. "He was crazy about you, too. Never understood how you could be so cold-hearted."

She fixed him with a dirty look. "C'mon, Al. I told you it wasn't like that."

"He wanted to marry you," he accused. "Bought a ring and everything."

"I caught him with some bimbo, Al," she blurted out. "In bed with some fan who was too stupid to realize he wasn't even a driver. Give me some credit here, please."

Al's face turned a deep scarlet. "He what?"

It was time he knew the truth; she was sick and tired of taking all the blame. "He cheated on me, Al," she said with a sigh. "And I caught him. That's all there was to it."

"Why the hell didn't you tell me this before now? I'd have kicked his ass to kingdom come, and you know it."

"And that's exactly why I didn't tell you. He's your nephew. Besides, it was embarrassing enough. I really didn't want to talk about it."

But even if Don *had* been faithful, she wouldn't have married him—not that she'd ever admit that to Al. They'd had some fun, but she couldn't imagine spending the rest of her life with him.

"It's a good thing that boy's in Florida right now," Al muttered, looking suitably outraged. "Otherwise I'd wring his scrawny neck. It's one thing if you didn't want to tell me the truth, but he sure as hell should have, the coward."

"C'mon, Al, it's old news now, anyway. Give him a break, why don't you?"

"I'm going to call him up tonight and have a little chat with him, that's all."

She couldn't help but smile, imagining how that conversation was going to go. "Be sure and tell him I said hi, why don't you?"

"Yeah, sure." He shook his head. "Well, what about Tieri? You gonna tell me the truth about him, at least? I'll kick his ass if he's done something to hurt you. That's the least I can do to make up for my sorry excuse for a nephew."

"Well, that's right nice of you, Al, but truly, he hasn't done anything to warrant it. Like I said, there's nothing going on between us."

"Yeah, you keep telling yourself that. Well, since you're here anyway, you might as well get to work. C'mon, I'll show you our newest data. Maybe you'll have some brilliant ideas for us."

She rubbed her hands together, anxious to get to work. "I usually do, don't I?" At the very least, it would take her mind off Damon.

CHAPTER ELEVEN

August, Watkins Glen, New York

"HEY, AL, I'M GOING out for a bit. If anyone comes looking for me, just play dumb, okay?"

Al set down his clipboard. "You mean Tieri?"

"Not specifically." Because she was pretty sure Damon was still avoiding her. "What part of *anyone* didn't you understand?"

"Awfully snippy today," he murmured. "Where are you running off to?"

"I thought I'd go into the village for a little bit," Shelly answered with a shrug. "Just to walk around some. Maybe I'll take Trixie with me, let her stretch her legs."

"Whatever you say." He glanced down at his watch. "Final practice is at five-thirty, though. Better be back in plenty of time."

"Don't worry, I will," Shelly said, lowering the brim of her ZippiPrint cap over her eyes. She had a couple of hours to kill, and she planned to make the best of it.

"Oh, and you might want to change that hat," Al

called out just as Shelly turned to leave. "If you want to go incognito, that is."

Hmm, he had a point. Maybe she could bum a Kyle Jordan hat off someone in his garage—that'd throw folks off the scent. Laughing at her own private joke, she hurried off toward Jordan's garage area.

Fifteen minutes later she went in search of a security van to drive her out. She tightened the blue cap on her head, thinking what a brilliant disguise it was. She'd planned on taking Trixie with her, but ultimately decided against it, mostly because there was no way to access the NASCAR Nationwide Series motor home lot without walking through a throng of race fans.

She wasn't leaving her anonymity to chance. Wearing jeans and a bright pink T-shirt, she hoped she could simply blend into the crowd that filled the quaint little village on race weekends.

There was a great little pet store on Franklin Street—she'd buy some gourmet dog treats for Trixie, and maybe get her a new collar, too. And then maybe she'd grab a slice of pizza at Jerlondo's before checking out Famous Brands, her favorite local clothing store.

The very idea of escaping the crowds and doing something totally mundane and mindless made her hurry her step in anticipation. She was so lost in her thoughts, humming some pop tune as she walked past the media center, that she barely heard her name called over the din of the crowd.

She turned, looking for the source of the voice, and saw Damon lift one hand in greeting. Great. Just the guy she *didn't* want to see. She had no idea where they stood personally, no idea where the sponsorship deal stood, either. But somehow she knew she wasn't going to get any answers, at least not right now.

Which meant they'd be forced to make polite conversation, instead. "Hey, Tieri," she called out, returning his wave, then turned back and continued on her way.

"Wait," he called out, jogging over to her side. "Where are you off to?"

"Out," she answered simply, in no mood for chit-chat.

"Out? Out where?"

She pointed off toward the rolling green hills in the distance. "Out there. The village, actually. Notice my disguise?" She spread her arms wide.

"Very clever," he said with an easy laugh, the corners of his dark eyes crinkling in that adorable way they did when he smiled. "I like the hat."

Don't let him get to you, she chastised herself. *He's not all that.*

"Yeah, I thought that was a nice touch. Anyway, I don't have a lot of time before final practice, so I better get going."

Damon nodded, then glanced down at his watch. "Hey, would you mind some company?" he asked, meeting her gaze once more. "I could give you a lift, have you back in plenty of time."

Shelly took a deep breath, considering her options. Refuse him, which was probably the smart thing to do. Or take him up on his offer, which seemed the polite thing to do. But what kind of message would that send?

That she was at his beck and call, ready to jump at any little bone he dangled in front of her?

On the other hand, what kind of message would refusing him send? That she was bothered by his seeming lack of interest, both personally and professionally? That he'd hurt her feelings? She was supposed to be playing it cool, after all. Letting him know he was getting under her skin seemed the height of *un*cool.

Truth was, just standing there next to him made her feel slightly breathless, her knees a little weak. Her senses seemed heightened, and every inch of her body was physically aware of his, only inches away. He had some weird physical effect on her, kind of like the adrenaline rush she felt behind the wheel of a race car. Whatever it was, it made him pretty darn hard to refuse.

Not that she really wanted to, if truth be told.

"Sure, why not?" she said at last, trying her best to remain completely unmoved by the movie-star smile that was her reward for agreeing. Why'd he have to go and do that, anyway? Dazzle her with that smile of his?

"Then c'mon, let's get out of here," he said. "Random Kyle Jordan fan," he added wryly, flicking the brim of her cap.

CHAPTER TWELVE

"HOW'S THE COFFEE?" Damon asked, smiling at the woman who sat beside him on a wooden bench, her blue eyes the exact same shade as the cap she wore pulled low over her brow.

"It's good," she murmured, watching him over the rim of her paper cup.

In front of them, Seneca Lake stretched out toward the horizon, its waters inky and still.

He knew he should have left her alone there at the track, should have watched her walk by without drawing attention to himself. And yet he hadn't been able to ignore her, hadn't been able to pass up the opportunity to spend some time with her. It had been a *long* couple of weeks.

So they'd strolled through the village's streets, stopping at shops to browse, acting like tourists for the better part of an hour before grabbing a slice of pizza and walking over to the pier.

Only now that they were done eating, conversation was proving awkward. They couldn't talk about the sponsorship, because there really wasn't anything to say. Missy Green showing up at the winery had pretty much knocked Shelly from contention, as far as he was concerned.

He felt badly about it, too. It wasn't Shelly's fault, and she shouldn't be held responsible for her mother's actions. But he had a business to run and a professional reputation to maintain. What if Shelly was participating in some sponsorship event—a commercial shoot, or a fan appreciation function—and her mother showed up, drunk and disorderly? At a *wine* business event, no less. It was a chance he wasn't prepared to take, no matter how much he liked her.

Her mother was a definite liability; right now, he couldn't see a way around it. But that didn't mean he wasn't still drawn to Shelly. Worse, he was sure that she thought he'd been an ass these past weeks. And maybe he *had* been an ass. He'd called her a couple of times, but he hadn't been quite sure what to say to her. This was entirely new territory for him, and nothing he did seemed right where she was concerned.

"You looked good at practice today," he said, deciding to stick to racing talk. It seemed the only safe option, which kind of made him sad.

"Yeah, my car is fast. Should be a good race tomorrow." She took a sip of her coffee.

"Road racing is different from the oval tracks. Almost seems like a totally different skill set."

"Yeah, you get to turn right for a change," she said wryly. "It's definitely challenging. Up and down hills, more shifting, heavier braking. Stuff like that. It's more about control than going full throttle like you do on a superspeedway, but you can be a little more aggressive."

"How so?" he asked, enjoying the way she educated him on the sport without talking down to him. He'd learned more from Shelly than he had from all the books he'd read about stock car racing put together.

"Well," she said, gazing out toward the lake, "for starters, you're not going that fast. Relatively speaking, of course. Which means you can be a little more persistent when you're trying to pass. Still, you've got to go all-out on qualifying. It's pretty hard to work your way through the field, so you don't want to start at the back. I actually like road racing a lot."

"I hear you're pretty good at it, too."

"Compliments will get you nowhere," she teased, and suddenly she seemed like herself again, the vivacious girl with the sharp wit. "Hey, did you notice the big courthouse in town? The Schuyler County Courthouse?" she asked.

"Yeah, I think so. Why?"

"Well, did you know that right in front of it is the start/finish line for the original Watkins Glen street circuit? Six-point-six miles, through town and into the countryside. Started in 1948, I think."

"Really? I didn't know that."

Shelly nodded. "Yeah, it's on the National Historic Registry and everything. Pretty cool stuff. You should check out the Motor Racing Research Center here if you get a chance. I'd take you there now, if we had time. They'll give you a map and you can follow the markers and drive the original course yourself."

"Maybe I'll go after I drop you back at the track," Damon said, thinking it sounded like a good way to kill some time.

"What, and miss the final practice session?"

"Probably wouldn't be the end of the world. I'm still trying to learn what I can about the sport, history included."

"Well, there's a lot of history here at the Glen. Trust me, the folks at the research center will be happy to talk your ear off about it."

"Sounds good to me," Damon said, crumpling his empty cup and tossing it into a nearby trash can.

"And he scores!" Shelly called out, making him chuckle.

"Lucky shot," he said, suddenly unable to take his eyes off her. The truth hit him like a punch in the gut—he'd missed her. *Badly.* Would she ever forgive him if he passed her over for the sponsorship? "I…uh, I'm sorry we haven't gotten a chance to talk much since Sonoma. It's just been a little crazy, all this traveling from track to track."

Shelly rolled her eyes, a smile tipping the corners of her mouth. "Yeah, welcome to my world. How are you getting around, anyway? Has Pebble Valley bought a plane yet?"

"No, we're still chartering Brent Sanford's. A plane's on my list, though. Maybe next year. Does Sanford Racing fly you back and forth?"

"Yeah. Only Sprint Cup drivers can afford their own planes. Successful Sprint Cup drivers," she amended with a shrug. "That's on my 'someday' list, too."

"So, how's your mother doing?" Damon asked, then wished he could take back the words. Shelly's eyes had instantly darkened, the light behind them dimming noticeably. "Steve says she sent him a really nice note," he added.

"She's doing good. Entered a program, doing the twelve-step thing and all that. It's weird, but we've actually talked more in these past couple of weeks than we have in years. I think maybe she's finally getting herself together. I guess you could say I'm cautiously optimistic."

"That's great. I'm really glad to hear it." He kept his gaze neutral, staring out at the lake.

"Yeah, and it turns out she knows a lot more about racing than she ever let on. Sometimes I forget…well, you know. With my father and all."

She'd never identified the man who'd fathered her, just said that he was a driver. "Do you know who your father is?" he asked, unable to staunch his curiosity. "You don't have to answer that if it makes you uncomfortable."

She shook her head. "No idea. I don't want to know, either. I mean, he knew my mom was pregnant when he walked out on her. He's probably done the math. Unless he's living under a rock, he must know who *I* am, and I don't see him knocking on my door." For the briefest of moments, her bravado slipped, and he saw pain flicker in her eyes.

Damon resisted the urge to reach out to her, to take her hand in his. Instead, he shoved his hands into his pockets, clenching them into fists of restraint. "As long as you're okay with that."

She brushed a lock of hair out of her eyes with the sweep of one hand. "I'm perfectly okay with it. I've done just fine without him all these years. What would be the point of pretending some stranger is part of my life?"

Damon shook his head. "I don't know. Just…medical history, maybe?"

"My mom's told me what she knows, as far as that goes. Anyway, I don't think about it too much."

"Huh. I think the curiosity would probably drive me nuts. There's so much information out there these days, with the Internet. You've never been tempted to do a little digging?"

"I try and stay away from the Internet," she said with a shrug. "Once I made the mistake of visiting a message board, you know, about me. God, it was awful, some of the stuff they were saying. Someone even swore that Kyle Jordan and I were an item, that they'd seen us together at a bar in Mooresville, making out on the dance floor." She mock shuddered. "As *if.*"

"That's a pretty horrifying image," he agreed.

"And then there was this one woman who claimed to be my biggest fan. She actually has this Shelly Green shrine in her house, you know, pictures, memorabilia, stuff I've signed. Says she picks four-leaf clovers and lights purple candles for me every weekend, and she talks about me like she knows me, like we're best friends or something. Totally creeped me out."

Shelly tipped her cup back, draining what was left in it. "Anyway, we should probably get back to the track."

"Probably so," Damon agreed reluctantly. "This has been nice, though."

"Yeah, I'm glad I let you twist my arm. You're pretty good company, Tieri. When you're not getting on my nerves, that is."

He threw back his head and laughed at that, remembering the philosophical discussion they'd had back in Daytona. "Ah, those were the days. Seems like just yesterday, doesn't it?"

It sounded like she muttered, "I think it *was* yesterday," but he couldn't be sure.

He raked one hand through his hair, wishing they could stay, wishing he could take her to dinner. Instead, he rose and offered his hand to help her up.

Just then a couple of guys—college students, by the looks of them—stopped beside them on the pier. "Hey, aren't you Shelly Green?" one of them asked, his voice filled with awe. "You know, the driver of the ZippiPrint car?"

Shelly acted quickly. "Shelly Green?" she said, her voice dripping with disdain. "Ugh, she's terrible. Kyle Jordan's the man." She pointed to her hat.

"Kyle Jordan's a jerk," the second guy offered.

Guy number one squinted his eyes, his gazing sweeping from the top of Shelly's head down to her feet, and then back up again, lingering a little too long on the place where the V-neck of her T-shirt dipped down, pulled low by a pair of folded sunglasses. "I swear, you look just like her," he said, finally looking at her face again.

Damon couldn't help but bristle, feeling somehow…

possessive. Which was oddly disturbing, since he'd never felt possessive of a woman before—particularly one he wasn't even dating.

Guy number two shook his head. "Nah, this chick's much prettier than Shelly Green. Bad taste in drivers, though. Paul Jackson's the one to watch in the NASCAR Nationwide Series."

Shelly just shrugged. "Jackson's okay, I guess."

Guy number one folded his arms across his chest. "Green's going to get the championship this year, though, just watch. She's awesome."

The second guy nudged his friend in the ribs. "Admit it, you're hot for her."

"Shut up, man. I'm telling you, she's got real talent. If it's got four tires and a steering wheel, she can drive the hell out of it. Just watch, she'll be in the Sprint Cup Series soon enough."

"You really think so?" Shelly asked, feigning surprise.

"Hell, yeah. She's better than half the guys already there."

"I couldn't agree more," Damon put in, checking his watch one more time. "I hate to interrupt, Shel—Sharon," he corrected, improvising, "but we've really got to go."

"Yeah, I guess we do. It was good chatting with you guys," Shelly said to her admirers. She waved goodbye, then started off, a bounce in her step that wasn't there before, an unmistakable grin on her face.

Damon was glad to see it, even if he hadn't been the one to put it there, even if he had some randy college boys to thank for it.

Someday, he told himself as he fell into step beside her, *I'm going to make her smile like that.* The hows and whys didn't matter, not right now. He just had to get through this season first, keep himself emotionally detached long enough to make his decision about the sponsorship. And after that, well…he could only hope that afterward Shelly would still give him the time of day.

WHAT THE HELL? IT felt like Kyle Jordan was trying to take her bumper off. Shelly glanced in her rearview mirror, watching as he plowed into her once more, sending her rear tires out from under her.

She fought the wheel, dragging the car back under control as she made her way through the bus-stop chicane, Jordan banging into her the whole way through. He was doing his best to spin her out into the gravel, the jerk. Payback for Chicago, she guessed.

Accelerating as she headed into the chute, she finally put some distance between her car and Jordan's. Her car was better than his today—faster. But that didn't matter much on a road course where bunching up was inevitable.

She had to brake again for Turn Seven, the so-called toe, and then downshift for Turn Eight, the "boot," heading uphill toward the straightaway just past Turn Nine. There were still twenty-two laps to go, and already her arms were killing her.

Just as she headed into the second-to-last turn, Jordan pulled his nose up to her right rear quarter panel and tapped her, sending her sliding sideways through the grass.

Cursing loudly, Shelly gripped the wheel, coaxing the car back under control, back onto the asphalt just in time for Turn Twelve. What the hell was Jordan doing? He was going to get black-flagged for aggressive driving if he kept it up. Was retaliation so important to him that he'd risk a good finish? If he got sent to the back of the line, he'd have no chance of working his way back up front again.

A cold sweat broke out on her forehead as she sped down the straightaway across the start/finish line and headed toward turn one, a full ninety degrees. "How many spots did I just lose, Al?"

"Five spots, Shelly. It's okay, we've got time." He sounded far more cool and collected than she felt.

As soon as she navigated the tricky turn and headed toward the esses—easily her favorite part of the track—she keyed her mike again, addressing her spotter this time. "Hey, Rick, go have a little chat with Jordan's spotter, why don't you."

"I sure will," came Rick's voice. He was stationed on the front straightaway between the start/finish line and Turn One, so he'd no doubt seen that little maneuver Jordan had pulled. Her second spotter, Tom, was up overlooking the straightaway after the esses, just before the bus stop.

"You tell him I'm going to have a word with the little punk if he keeps it up," Al said, sounding more than a little annoyed. "We've got a yellow flag. Someone's stalled on the track."

"Just after Turn Four," Tom said. "The No. 502 Car, sitting down low on the track."

"Got it." Shelly sighed, grateful for the reprieve. Jordan had made her so mad that she'd lost her focus, lost the rhythm she'd found. "Are we going to pit this time around?" she asked.

"Just follow the leaders, Shel. If they pit, then come on in behind them."

"Ten-four. What position is Jordan in right now?"

"Looks like he's in fifth now," came Al's reply.

Shelly groaned. *Just great.* She was sitting in eleventh, just outside the top ten without a lot of time to work her way back up again.

But three laps later, things were looking up. There was a multi-car crash in the chicane, leaving four of the top-ten cars stuck in the gravel, Kyle Jordan included. She almost laughed as she drove by, thinking maybe there was something to the whole karma theory. *You reap what you sow,* she thought.

When the green flag waved again, Shelly had moved up to the sixth spot, thanks to an excellent pit stop. Two laps later, she'd managed to pick off two more cars. With four to go, one of the rookies wrecked in Turn Three, necessitating a green-white-checker finish.

The car directly in front of Shelly spun its tires on the restart, allowing Shelly to squeak by into the third spot, and that's where she took the checkered flag.

"We'll take it, Shelly," Al said as she cruised past the start/finish line.

"You bet we will," she replied. "Way to go, guys. That last pit stop saved us."

"Doesn't hurt to have the best road-course driver out there, either," Al said, his voice full of obvious pride.

Shelly couldn't help but smile at that. She was definitely moving on up, as they liked to say.

NASCAR Sprint Cup Series, here I come. With or without Pebble Valley Winery. Unfortunately, it looked liked she'd have to do without.

CHAPTER THIRTEEN

August, Brooklyn, Michigan

"JUST HIT YOUR MARKS, SHELLY," came Al's voice in her headset. "You've got this one, I just know it."

"From your lips to God's ears," Shelly murmured, gripping the wheel tight as she guided the car onto the track and accelerated, keeping her gaze locked on the asphalt in front of her.

She mentally ran through the track's stats as she picked up speed, gaining momentum, preparing to take her two qualifying laps. Shelly loved the superspeedways, loved the high speeds, the strategy involved.

A track like this was all about aerodynamics, and they'd spent some time in the wind tunnel preparing for today's race, making changes. She'd felt sure they'd figured some things out, and two excellent practice sessions had proved her right—she'd clocked the fastest speed in the final practice session yesterday, and now she was going to nail her qualifying run—she could just feel it.

Going wide open on the throttle, she rocketed past

the start/finish line, gripping the wheel as she guided the car through Turns One and Two, then down the long backstretch, picking up speed as she went.

"One-eighty-five-point-six," came Al's voice in her ear. "Keep it up—just hit those marks."

She sped through Turns Three and Four, her jaw clenched with concentration as she flew past the start/finish line once more, everything a blur.

"One-eighty-six-point-seven," Al said quietly, and Shelly knew that was good, *real* good. There was total radio silence as she completed her second lap.

But as soon as she crossed the start/finish line and let off the throttle, Al began to whoop it up. "Yee-haw! You just took the pole and set a track record, too! Woo-hoo!"

Yes! Shelly banged on the steering wheel with one fist. Things were looking up, everything falling into place neatly now. A third-place finish at Watkins Glen, and now a possible pole there at Michigan. There were only a half-dozen cars left to qualify, none of them any real competition, not when she'd set a qualifying record.

Coasting now, she pulled off the track and headed toward the garage. Pulling into her stall, she cut the motor and sat there, content inside the car's cockpit, wanting to savor the moment alone for a bit before she joined her teammates in celebration.

This is what it's all about, she reminded herself as she removed her helmet. Not about sponsorships or corporate endorsements—not even about the money. It was all about the feeling inside her right then—the adrenaline, the rush of excitement that electrified her, made her feel exceptionally alive.

It didn't matter that Damon was there at the track, a guest of Kyle Jordan's team again. Rumor had it that Jordan's team owner had dropped the price of a sponsorship. Apparently they'd secured a substantial secondary sponsor. At this point, Jordan would be a bargain for Pebble Valley Winery, but Shelly reminded herself that that didn't matter, either.

What mattered was that her ZippiPrint team was the best team in the NASCAR Nationwide Series. Even now, they surrounded the car, high-fiving and laughing as they waited for her to drop the net and climb out.

Taking one last, fortifying breath, she did just that. As soon as her feet hit the concrete, Al lifted her up, twirling her around while he crowed and cheered, the entire team joining in, clapping her on the shoulder as she went past.

"C'mon, enough already!" she said with a laugh, stumbling when Al sat her back unsteadily on her feet. "Save the celebrating for after I win, why don't you?"

She stumbled back against something solid, gasping when hands clamped down on her shoulders, steadying them. "Whoa," an all-too-familiar voice said.

She spun around too fast, nearly tripping over her own feet in the process.

"I had to come and congratulate you," Damon said, looking model-perfect in a pair of crisp khakis and white linen shirt, the sleeves rolled up to his elbows. "That qualifying run was something else."

"Yeah, thanks," she murmured, thinking only Damon could pull off a look like that at a race track.

"I, uh—" he glanced around at her team who milled around, trying to look as if they weren't listening to every word he was saying "—I was wondering if you'd like to have dinner with me tonight. After the race. It's not—" he glanced around once more, then lowered his voice an octave "—not business-related, not exactly. There's just something I'd like to discuss with you. In private," he added.

Shelly swallowed hard, wishing he'd saved the invitation till later. Till after the race. The last thing she needed was to get distracted, wondering what he wanted to talk to her about.

The likely answer was that he was choosing Kyle Jordan for the Pebble Valley sponsorship. It would be just like Damon to want to tell her first, in person. Make him feel noble and all that.

On the other hand, he did say it wasn't business-related, so that probably ruled out anything pertaining to the sponsorship deal. Which just made his invitation all the more intriguing.

"Sure," she said at last. "Why not?"

Truth was, she could think of a million reasons why not. Only problem was, she didn't really care, not with him standing next to her.

SHELLY SLIPPED INTO THE chair opposite Damon's, glad she'd worn one of the skirts and blouses she'd bought with Becky. When he'd asked her to dinner, she'd assumed he'd take her someplace nice, near the track. Instead, he'd taken her all the way out to Ann Arbor, to a swanky French restaurant with a name she couldn't even pronounce.

Damon had exchanged his linen shirt for a more tailored one, but he hadn't worn a tie. It didn't really matter, though, because Damon could fit in just about anywhere, no matter how he was dressed. It was all in his attitude, she realized.

And that attitude was starting to rub off on her, she noticed as she accepted the menu the white-jacketed maître d' handed her. Six months ago, she would have been uncomfortable at a restaurant like this, imagining everyone staring at her. After all, the 'Bama Café back in her hometown was more her speed.

But now this felt almost like an adventure, an experience to savor, to learn from. And she wanted to learn, to expand her horizons. Truth was, she wasn't that small-town girl from Alabama anymore. She had to stop pretending she was, clinging to that identity, to those old insecurities.

Damon glanced up at her and smiled, and she smiled back. There had been no hint of the meaning behind tonight's dinner on the drive over. They'd talked about the race, about her second-place finish that had left a bad taste in her mouth, considering she had definitely had the winning car.

One of her rear-tire changers had made a costly mistake, and she'd had to make an unscheduled pit stop to tighten a lug nut. She'd managed to stay on the lead lap after that, but had to fight her way back through traffic, picking them off one at a time. There just hadn't been time to get back up front.

Kyle Jordan's day had been worse, though, so that softened the blow a bit.

"Would you mind if I ordered for us both?" Damon asked, and Shelly just shrugged. Turns out the menu was in French, and she couldn't make out more than a word or two, anyway. It would be interesting to see what he selected.

"How do you feel about escargot in garlic oil?" he asked after a minute or two, glancing up with a hopeful look on his face.

She decided to go for honesty. "Pretty nauseated by the whole idea, to tell you the truth. But don't let it stop you from enjoying them," she added.

"How about lobster bisque, then?"

"That's much more my speed," she said with a nod. It sounded good, actually.

"Great. Do you eat duck?"

"C'mon, Tieri. I'm a meat-and-three kind of girl."

"Meat-and-three?"

She shook her head, remembering her earlier resolve. "Never mind. You know what? Surprise me. I'm feeling kind of adventurous. Just…not the snails." A shudder worked its way down her spine.

"I thought I'd get a bottle of wine, too. Something you might like. But if you'd prefer a soda—"

"No, wine sounds good," she interrupted. "Really," she added. He looked so…earnest.

The waiter finally appeared. Shelly watched while Damon ordered, amazed as always by his competence, his cool confidence. He seemed so sure of everything he did, as if self-doubt never crossed his mind. Of course, she liked to think of herself that way, too—as a driver. But as a woman?

If only she knew what he was thinking. Did she baffle him as much as he baffled her? Theirs was a strange relationship, after all. It wasn't like they were dating, at least not in the true sense of the word. And yet, almost every time they were together, it felt like a date. Heck, tonight felt like a date.

What in the world did he want to talk to her about, if not the sponsorship deal?

"You're quiet tonight," he said when the waiter left.

"Still licking my wounds," she lied, figuring it was as good an excuse as any. "I hate to lose like that."

His brow furrowed above his dark eyes. "You finished second, Shelly. Not too shabby for a day's work."

"Second isn't good enough, not if you want to win a championship. And not when you've got as good a car as I had today. You have to take advantage of an opportunity like that."

The waiter reappeared then, bearing a bottle of wine. He poured a small amount in Damon's glass, then stood watching while Damon took a sip and nodded. With a flourish, the waiter filled Shelly's glass then Damon's before taking his leave.

Damon raised his glass, swirling the pale-yellow

liquid around. "It's a Sauvignon blanc from the Loire Valley, light and fruity. I think you might like it," he said.

Shelly took a sip, surprised to find that he was right. "It's good. Sort of tastes like pears. Maybe grapefruit, too."

A slow smile spread across his face. "That's exactly the flavors in this particular vintage. I'm impressed."

"I guess that afternoon spent in Pebble Valley's tasting room paid off."

"It would seem so," he said, looking genuinely pleased. "You're a quick study. I ordered you an endive salad with goat cheese. It'll pair up nicely, just wait."

"You're the expert," she said with a shrug, just as the waiter appeared with said salad.

Which was delicious, she realized, with walnuts and dried cranberries. Next came soup—a rich, fragrant bisque with chunks of lobster. As soon as that was cleared away, the waiter brought several steaming plates—duck, salmon and beef burgundy, it turned out. All mouth-wateringly delicious.

She had to give Damon credit where credit was due. "You sure know your way around a menu, Tieri," she said as the waiter cleared away the plates and refilled their wineglasses. Shelly was surprised to see that hers had been empty. Had she really drank that much? Maybe that was why her skin felt so flushed, her limbs so loose.

"I enjoy eating out way too much," he said with a grimace. "It's why I had to take up jogging."

"You jog? In New York City?"

"Sure, in the park. Central Park," he clarified. "Right

across the street from my apartment. I hate it, to tell you the truth. Jogging, I mean. A necessary evil."

"Huh. Well, you could always go to the gym, instead."

He shook his head. "No way. That just seems so…artificial."

That was an interesting way of looking at it. "Yeah, I guess it is. Still, it's a necessity in NASCAR, you know. I work out every day. In a gym," she clarified. "Just jogging alone wouldn't cut it."

"No, I guess it wouldn't. I admit, I was surprised to learn that drivers are such serious athletes. The endurance required—" he shook his head "—it's mind-boggling, really."

She shrugged. "Well, you learn quickly that keeping yourself in shape makes your day all that much easier behind the wheel."

He nodded, leaning back in his chair. For a moment he said nothing; he simply stared at her, watching her intently.

"Why'd you bring me here tonight?" she blurted out. "You said you wanted to talk to me about something. Honestly, it's driving me crazy wondering just what that something is."

"I'm sorry," he said. "I've been trying all night to work up the nerve." He glanced over his shoulder at the waiter, who was headed their way with what must be dessert.

Shelly just stared at him while the waiter arranged the plates and poured coffee. Damon, needing to work up courage? It didn't compute—he was way too self-assured, confident to the point of arrogance. It was part of his charm, really.

At last the waiter left, and they were alone again.

"So," Damon began, pushing away his dessert plate untouched. "First off, I want you to know that I'm not rushing into any decision regarding the sponsorship. I know I said this wasn't about business, but I wanted to get that out the way first. I have to make the decision that's right for Pebble Valley Winery." He paused, taking a sip of coffee, looking entirely uncomfortable, almost pained. "I can't let my…feelings…impact that decision," he finished.

Just what was he trying to say? "What feelings are you talking about, Damon?" she pressed.

"My feelings for you, Shelly," he said roughly, looking somehow tortured. "Strong feelings. I don't think I've ever quite felt this way about anyone before. I know you think I'm a complete jackass—"

"No, I don't," she interrupted. "At least, not always."

"It didn't seem right not to tell you," he continued on, as if she hadn't spoken, as if he were in a rush to spill it all out. "I've had to try and keep my distance, because of the whole sponsorship thing, but I thought you deserved to know why. And I thought you needed to know how difficult it's been for me."

"When you say strong feelings…" She trailed off, clearing her throat, trying to tamp down the hope that had blossomed in her heart, making it pound furiously. "What exactly do you mean by that?"

Again, pain flitted across his face. This was clearly difficult for him. Which didn't make sense to her, not really. Here she was, restraining herself from jumping up and throwing her arms around him, and he just looked like a drowning man.

"I don't know," he said at last, shaking his head. "But from the moment I met you, it's like there was this connection or something. A spark. I broke up with Courtney, you know. Right after Daytona."

No, she hadn't known that; at least, not for certain. She'd always wondered if the faceless Courtney was still waiting in the wings, ready to reclaim her man. That was part of the reason she'd never really allowed herself to hope—

"Just one kiss, and I felt something stronger for you than I've ever felt for her—for anyone, for that matter. I knew then it wasn't right, wasn't meant to be. With Courtney, I mean."

Wow. *Wow.* That word kept repeating itself, over and over in her mind. She was stunned—all this time, she'd tried to suppress her own blossoming feelings for Damon. Because, despite their obvious physical attraction, she'd never allowed herself to actually believe that he'd felt the same way about her as she did about him.

Like the whole twelve-step thing with her mom, it just seemed too good to be true. Which—again—usually meant that it was. After all, they were from different worlds, and more than just geographically speaking.

"Please tell me that this isn't totally one-sided, Shelly. You *do* feel something for me, too, don't you?" he asked, his voice low. He seemed so unsure of himself, so vulnerable.

This was a totally different Damon, and it made her

feel a little off-balance. She swallowed a lump in her throat. "It's not just you, Damon. I feel the same way. But...what do we do now?"

"We go back to Mooresville and wait it out, I guess. I'm renting a place out on Lake Norman now."

"Really? I didn't know that." Apparently there was a lot she didn't know.

"It's just temporary, till the end of the season. I wanted to be near the race shops."

"Okay, so we go back to Mooresville," Shelly agreed, nodding. "Then what?"

He shook his head. "I really don't know, Shelly. I wish I did, but right now, the sponsorship deal has to take precedence."

"Of course," she murmured.

"And until that's all worked out, we should probably keep our distance."

"So you won't be influenced," she said with a nod.

"Yeah, partly. But it's more than that, and you know it." He sighed loudly, then gestured for the check. "No matter what happens, I don't want anyone to say that our personal relationship influenced my decision. That wouldn't be fair to you."

"You're right," she agreed. Everything he said made perfect sense. Really, there wasn't any other solution. No matter what they felt, they needed to take a step back. To gain some perspective. To figure out exactly what it was they wanted from each other. A friendship? A fling? Or something more than that.

Still, she couldn't help the disappointment that

washed over her. They enjoyed each other's company—there was no point in denying that. She didn't really want to take a step back. Relationships were kind of like racing, after all. Things were pretty easy once you were up front, sailing through the clean air.

But if you dropped back in traffic, well, things got in the way. Your car changed. The track changed. And this definitely felt like dropping back in traffic, giving up the clean air.

"I guess we've got really bad timing, huh?" she said at last.

"I guess we do," he agreed.

CHAPTER FOURTEEN

GATHERING TRIXIE IN her lap, Shelly sat down on the couch next to Missy, surprised at how healthy her mother looked. She'd dropped a few pounds since she'd seen her last in Sonoma, and her face seemed thinner, less bloated.

"So, how's it going, Ma?" she asked, glancing around Missy's living room. It was tidy, neat. Decorated in what Missy liked to call "country casual," with teddy bears strewn around, hand-knitted doilies on every available surface. Framed photos of Shelly lined the wall behind the couch, beginning with her gap-toothed kindergarten picture and ending with a shot from last year of Shelly posing beside the ZippiPrint car, her helmet in one hand.

"I haven't had a drink in three weeks," Missy answered, her voice full of pride. "Joyce—that's my sponsor—says I'm doing great. I think you'd like her."

"I'm proud of you, Ma," Shelly said, fighting back tears. "Really. I wasn't sure you could do it."

"I took on another shift at the Grocery Barn, too. I'm cuttin' back at the track. Joyce doesn't think it's the right environment for me right now, and she's probably right," Missy said with a laugh.

"Like I said, just one day at a time. You sure you don't want to come to Atlanta with me for the weekend?"

"I wish I could, but Joyce says it's better if I stick close to home for now. You know, establish a routine. I think I might get myself a dog. Something small, like Trixie." She reached out to scratch the dog under her chin. "She's such a cute little thing," Missy said, as if she were speaking to a child.

"I think a dog's a great idea. You should go check out the shelter, see what they've got."

"I heard a rumor that they're naming their new building after you, you know. The Shelly Green Animal Center, they call it."

Shelly smiled, thinking she'd stop by on her way out of town and check it out. She'd made a sizable donation to the shelter last year. It was where she'd found Trixie—poor little thing's hair had been a mass of knots, and she'd been jumping with fleas when she'd first laid eyes on her. But it had been love at first sight, she thought, stroking the little dog.

If only every relationship were as easy as this one. Dogs were so easy to love, so quick to love you back. It was so simple, so black and white. She sighed deeply, remembering her conversation with Damon over dinner in Michigan. All her doubts about him had crowded back in. There was no black and white where Damon was concerned—it was all shades of gray.

And she had to face the facts. The relationship

wasn't something she could just make happen, no matter how badly she wanted it. And she *did* want it badly, she realized.

One tear escaped her suddenly brimming eyes, rolling down her cheek before she had the chance to wipe it away.

"Okay, out with it," Missy said, settling back against the couch's cushions with a knowing look. "It's a man, isn't it?"

Shelly feigned ignorance. "What are you talking about? I've just got something in my eye, that's all. Probably dog hair."

"Oh, come off it. You know exactly what I'm talking about, Michelle Elizabeth Green. Don't forget, I raised you. Who is it, and what'd he do to you?"

Shelly let out her breath in a rush, surprised at how perceptive her mother was. She might as well tell her the truth; it wasn't like she had anyone else to talk to about it. "Remember Damon Tieri?" she asked. "Tall, dark? You met him in Daytona and again in Sonoma."

Missy raised her brows suggestively. "How could I forget? The Italian Stallion."

Shelly had to laugh at that. "Yeah, that's the one."

"The man's all sleek and classy. Anyway, I knew something was up with you two."

"Well, it wasn't then. Not really. It's just been…oh, I don't know, slowly simmering since we met. At first it was just physical."

"Oooh, this gets even better!" Missy squealed, clasping her hands together.

Shelly rolled her eyes heavenward. "Not like that. I

kissed him, that's all. A couple of times, and that's the extent of it. What kind of girl do you take me for?"

Missy raised one brow. "Obviously one who's not like her mama."

Shelly decided to ignore that. *Way too much information.* "Anyway, I told you about the Pebble Valley sponsorship, right? Well, he's the one making the final call. So he thinks he's got to keep his distance from me, not let his feelings for me influence his decision."

"Well, what's wrong with that? Let him make his decision, and then you can grab him."

Shelly shook her head, hating the tears that threatened to fall, burning behind her eyelids. "It's so much more complicated than that. First off, what if he doesn't choose me? For the sponsorship, I mean. What's that say about his feelings for me? I'm the best driver in the series, and he knows it. He doesn't think I'm right for Pebble Valley because I'm not classy enough. Not cultured enough, or something like that."

"In other words, he thinks you're some unsophisticated simpleton."

"That's pretty much it," Shelly said glumly. It sounded even worse when her mom put it that like that. She definitely had a way with words, though. "But I've been working on my polish. It's part of the business, really, and I can't expect to be a spokesperson without a bit of shine."

"Well, screw him, then," Missy said, patting her daughter's arm as though she was a child. "If he doesn't pick you, you tell him to stick it where the sun don't shine. There'll be other sponsors."

Trixie jumped down from Shelly's lap, curling up on the carpet at Shelly's feet, her little black nose resting on her paws. The perfect example of unconditional love.

"It's just that we come from such different worlds, Ma. He's from this…this big, happy family. They run this Wall Street business, managing money. He's really rich, really educated. Ivy League and all that."

"What's he doing nosin' around in NASCAR?"

"I don't know. He likes it, I guess. Seems genuinely interested in the sport. He likes *me,* too."

"But I thought you just said—"

"I know, I know. But he *does* like me, despite all that. He, quote—" she made little quotation marks in the air "—feels things for me that he's never felt for anyone else. End quote."

"Well, that's all fine and dandy for him. But what about you? How do you feel about him? Just 'cause he's got a thing for you doesn't mean you have to like him back."

Shelly sighed, dropping her gaze to her hands, studying her stained fingernails, the pink polish long chipped away. Becky would shudder in horror if she saw her now, after all the work she'd put into her.

"That's just it, Ma. I *do* like him back. A lot."

Missy curled her lower lip. "Really? Because he sounds like a jerk to me."

Shelly shook her head. "He's not a jerk. He's smart and funny and really kind of sweet. I guess you could call him arrogant, but really, it's just confidence. Because he's good at what he does, you know? And really, people probably call me arrogant, too, at least at the track. I don't have much problem tooting my own horn. So who am I to criticize?"

"But?" Missy prodded.

"But…I don't know. Whenever I'm around him, I can't think straight."

"Because he's sexy as all get out," Missy prompted.

That pretty much summed it up. "Yeah, he is. Am I really as shallow as that?" Shelly asked with a groan.

Missy shrugged. "Didn't you just say he was smart and funny and whatever other googly stuff you said? How's that shallow? The way I see it, the fact that he makes you all hot and bothered is just icing on the cake."

Shelly glanced sidelong at her mother, trying not to laugh. "I can't believe I'm getting relationship advice from you, of all people."

"Well, maybe I just don't want you to make the same mistake as I did. If you love him, then fight for him. Don't let him just walk out of your life."

Realization dawned on Shelly, taking her by surprise. "You really loved my dad, didn't you? It's why you never dated anyone else, never got married."

"Once I gave my heart to your daddy, there was no giving it away again."

"But…but he walked out on you," she sputtered. "On us."

"And I let him walk out. Acted like I didn't really care, one way or the other. I made it way too easy. He was young, he wasn't ready to be strapped down with a family."

"Well, he should've thought about that before—"

"Oh, I'm not excusin' him." Missy waved one hand

in dismissal. "Selfish son of a bitch. I'm just sayin' if I had a do-over, I'd have fought harder to hold on to him, that's all. I would have let him know how I really felt, and not let my pride get in the way."

"Huh." Shelly reached down to scratch a mosquito bite on her ankle. They always got her on the ankles.

"So, what do you think? You going to learn a lesson from your ol' ma and fight for your man?"

"Maybe I will," Shelly answered with a smile. "I haven't quite decided if he's worth it yet."

"Good. You make him earn it, hear me? Anyway, you want some tea? I didn't mean to sit here and chew your ear off."

"You got sweet tea?"

"What kind of place do you think this is? 'Course I do. You staying for dinner?"

"Depends on what you're cooking."

"I was kinda hoping that my fancy race-car driver of a daughter would treat me to dinner down at the 'Bama Café. You know, let me show you off some."

No way she was turning that down. It was only a four-hour drive back to Atlanta. She could probably make it three and a half, if she drove fast enough.

"You're on," Shelly said, feeling happier than she'd felt in weeks.

AN HOUR OUTSIDE Atlanta, Shelly's cell phone on the console between the car's front seats started ringing. She fumbled with her earpiece, looping it over her ear before hitting the button and connecting the call.

"What's up, boss?" she asked, noting Adam Sanford's name on the caller ID.

"Where are you?" he barked out.

"On I-20, headed toward the track. Why, what's wrong?"

His voice was grim. "We've got a problem, Shelly. You've got to pull double duty this weekend. I need you to drive for Trey."

"What? What happened? Is he okay?" Her words were rushing over each over in panic.

"He's fine. He just needs a…a procedure done over the weekend. Personal business. We'll probably need you in Richmond, too."

"Sure," she murmured, her worry for Trey battling with excitement over the opportunity to start in her first NASCAR Sprint Cup race. "Is this definite? Or is this like Indy when you put me on stand-by, just in case?"

They'd told her then that Trey had some sort of family emergency—which seemed weird at the time considering Trey's family was Adam's family, too. Adam even had her run some practice laps in Trey's car, but then Trey had shown up, after all.

"It's definite this time. We've already got someone working on a uniform for you," Adam continued, "and we'll have a seat made for you by tomorrow. They just want to take some new measurements. How soon till you get here?"

"About an hour, maybe less." This was her big chance, an opportunity to prove that she had what it takes to make it in the NASCAR Sprint Cup Series.

"Okay," Adam said, and Shelly could hear the strain in his voice. Trey Sanford was his brother, after all. The blood tie no doubt compounded whatever worry he felt as a team owner. He must be going crazy, she realized. "Come straight to the team hauler when you get here, Shelly."

"I will," she said, just before the line went dead.

Dear God, she hoped that whatever was wrong with Trey wasn't serious. Hitting the accelerator, she sped toward Atlanta, praying that she wouldn't let her team down.

DAMON FLIPPED OFF the TV in his hotel room, staring up at the ceiling in the darkness. Steve Clayton had just called him with the news that Shelly was going to drive Trey Sanford's Greenstone Garden Centers car in the NASCAR Sprint Cup Series race on Sunday. No one Steve had spoken with had known exactly what had happened to Trey, only that he'd be out for a couple of weeks and that Shelly would have to pull double duty for Sanford Racing in Atlanta and Richmond.

He was happy for her. She deserved this chance, even though he hated that she had to get it this way. He knew her well enough to know that her worry for her teammate's well-being would dampen her enjoyment of this professional milestone. Still, if she did well, everyone would be talking about her, and it would certainly silence her critics, the ones who didn't think that a female could hold her own in the NASCAR Sprint Cup Series. It was definitely going to be an interesting race weekend, no doubt about it.

He had considered inviting his family down. It was Labor Day, and he had thought it might be nice to get everyone together and introduce them to the sport. But mostly he'd wanted to introduce them to Shelly.

But then, coward that he was, he'd chickened out. All those unflattering things he'd thought about Shelly initially—those snobbish, prejudiced notions he'd had about someone from her background—his parents would think those same things, and much, much worse.

It'd be Tricia, all over again, only this would be worse, because when Mario had married Tricia, there had still been hope, as far as his parents were concerned. In their eyes, Damon was destined to right Mario's wrongs, to do the right thing by the family. He would find a woman they deemed appropriate and settle down, give them a houseful of little Tieris to carry on the family name and legacy—to walk the halls of Princeton and eventually take over the reins of TCM. That was their dream. And once he introduced them to Shelly, that dream would die a quick and painful death.

Only now that he thought about it, he didn't really care. The realization hit him like a ton of bricks. He didn't care, and that was the truth. And not caring… well, it felt pretty damn good, actually. He took a deep breath, surprised at how free he suddenly felt. It didn't matter what his parents thought. Their disappointment wouldn't affect his happiness, not unless he allowed it to.

The revelation was startling, yet comforting. In many ways, he'd been heading toward it for months now. He'd left the fund, invested in the winery and involved himself in a sport that his family knew nothing about. He'd even begun to distance himself from the family's charitable trust over the past few weeks, shifting some of his responsibilities to his sisters. Bit by bit, he'd been throwing off the yoke, and finding himself in the process.

The changes within him had been subtle, yet substantial, he realized. What that meant, exactly, he wasn't quite sure. Hell, at that moment, he wasn't sure of anything, except that it was going to be one hell of a race on Sunday. He couldn't help but wonder how Shelly was holding up under what must be an extraordinary amount of pressure.

There's one way to find out. He had her cell number, programmed in his phone. He could give her a call, offer her some moral support. Why not?

Flipping on the bedside light, he reached for his cell, unplugging it from its charger. He scrolled through the numbers, searching for hers. When he found it, he glanced at the clock, mentally debating whether or not it was too late. He'd be willing to bet she was still up. *What the hell,* he decided, looping his headset over his ear and hitting the button to connect the call.

She answered on the second ring. "Damon?"

"How'd you know it was me?" he asked, grinning like the proverbial schoolboy.

"Uh…ever heard of caller ID?" she asked, as sarcastic as ever.

"Oh. Yeah." He raked a hand through his hair, not quite sure how to proceed. "I…uh, heard the news. About Sunday. You ready?"

"Of course I'm ready." The enthusiasm in her voice was unmistakable. "Feels like I've been waiting forever for an opportunity like this. I just wish Trey—" She broke off with a sigh. "I just wish it wasn't at his expense. He's had a bad enough season as it is. Things were just starting to improve, and now this."

Damon heard Trixie barking in the background, and raised his voice to be heard over the din. "What's going on? With Trey, I mean. Steve didn't know."

"Shush, Trixie!" Shelly's voice was muffled, as if she'd covered the phone with one hand. "Sorry about that. She's been jumpy all night. I guess she can sense my excitement or something. Anyway, I have no idea what's going on with Trey. No one's telling me anything except I'm definitely going to be driving for him come Sunday. Crazy, isn't it?"

"Sure is. I'm looking forward to it." A knock sounded on his door.

"Turn down?" a voice called out.

"Nah, I'm fine," he yelled out.

"Where are you?" Shelly asked.

"My hotel," he answered, sitting back down on the side of the bed.

"Let me guess—the ritzest one downtown?" she said with a laugh.

"Something like that," he muttered, staring at the pad of paper beside the lamp with the hotel name written in heavy script. "I…uh, actually had some business to do, so I came down a day early and stayed downtown."

"I was just teasing you," she said, her voice laced

with amusement. "Most of the team sponsors are probably staying there, too. I can't help it, though. You're such easy prey."

"Hey, what can I say?"

"Actually, I was expecting you to tell me that you just liked the restaurant or something."

He cleared his throat, prepared to use his best stuffy investment banker voice. "Well, their muffins *are* exceptional."

"Yeah, and a station wagon's a very *safe* car," she countered.

"Hey, it *is* a safe car," he protested.

"You crack me up, Tieri." The tinkling sound of her laughter came through his earpiece.

"I'm glad," he said softly, surprised at the emotion he felt. Time to get back to neutral territory, and fast. "Looks like the last two races went really well for you. I'd planned to go to Bristol, but I ended up back in New York for business, instead. Lousy timing."

"Yeah, I'm sorry you missed it. I had a good two weeks. A fourth-place finish in Bristol and second in Montreal. I'm usually good in Montreal, but that's my best-ever finish at Bristol. I'm back at first in points now."

"Well, that's what counts, right?"

"In points racing, it does. It's too bad you missed Bristol, though. It's a great track."

"So they tell me." He glanced at the clock, knowing he should probably let her get some sleep. "Hey, I should let you go. You've got a busy weekend, pulling double duty."

"Don't I know it," she agreed. "A lot of the Sprint Cup guys do it all the time, though, so I can't complain too much."

"You, complaining? I know you're dying to get behind the wheel of that car and show them what you've got."

"Hey, you're staying through Sunday, right?"

"Yeah, I'm staying. I wouldn't miss your big debut."

"Whew! I just thought…well, anyway, I should get to bed. I'm glad you called, though."

Yeah, so am I. "See you tomorrow."

"It won't be hard to spot me. You know, since I'm the only girl out there and all."

Damon couldn't help but laugh at that. "That does make it easier," he said. "'Night, Shel."

"'Night, Damon."

The phone went quiet, though Damon's mind was anything but.

CHAPTER FIFTEEN

September, Atlanta, Georgia

SHELLY STOOD JUST OUTSIDE the Sanford Racing hauler, hoping that the pre-race reporters were done with her—for now, at least. They hadn't given her a moment's peace since she stepped out of the drivers' meeting, asking her the same questions, over and over again: *Are you excited about your first-ever NASCAR Sprint Cup Series start? Feeling any nerves right now? Are you feeling more confident after your second-place finish in the NASCAR Nationwide Series race yesterday?*

Yes, yes and no. She'd admitted to the nerves—after all, who wouldn't be nervous? But the truth was, no one had any idea just how nervous she was. She felt light-headed. Queasy, even.

What if she screwed up? What if she made some stupid mistake at a hundred and eighty miles per hour and wrecked the field? The list of possibilities was endless, and the more she thought about it, the more scared she became.

After all, she'd spent the better part of the season

trying to convince anyone who would listen that she was ready for the NASCAR Sprint Cup Series. If she messed up, that would be the end of it, would prove that she wasn't ready, after all. Chances like this didn't come along all that often, and it would be just her luck to screw it up now, when she'd come so close.

She took a deep, steadying breath, glancing down at the unfamiliar blue racing uniform she wore, trying to fight back the panic.

C'mon, get it together. You can do this.

"Hey, Shelly, it's almost time."

She glanced up to see Ethan Hunt striding her way wearing a uniform that matched the one she wore. Ethan was Trey's crew chief—*her* crew chief today.

"Hey, what's wrong?" Ethan asked, stepping closer. "You're looking a little green around the gills, if you don't mind my saying so."

Several members of Trey's team—her team, she corrected herself—began to gather around them, closing a circle that made her feel somehow claustrophobic.

"I—I'm fine," she stuttered, finding it hard to catch her breath. Good God, what was happening? She'd never lost it like this before a race, not once. "Really, I'm just…" she trailed off, unable to finish the sentence. Just what? Freaking out? Having a panic attack?

"Someone get her some water," Ethan barked.

She could feel it then, the panic spreading through the team as they all gaped at her, not quite sure what to say or do to snap her out of it.

Someone handed her a bottle of water and she gulped

it down, almost choking. Wiping her mouth on her sleeve, she took several deep breaths—in through her nose, out through her mouth. She knew she had to calm herself, to get her head on straight before she made a total idiot of herself right there in front of the team.

"There you are," came a familiar, deep voice.

Damon, just in time to witness her complete humiliation. *Great. What else?*

"I wanted to come over and wish you luck," he said, and the crowd of blue uniforms parted, making way for him. As soon as her panicked gaze met his, his eyes darkened a hue, his brow furrowed with concern. "Hey, what's wrong?"

Shelly just stood there, entirely mute.

"I think she's having a full-on panic attack or something," Ethan offered. "Why don't you take her inside the hauler, try and calm her down, talk some sense into her."

"Sure," he said.

As if on cue, the team retreated, leaving them all alone. Wordlessly, she followed Damon inside the hauler to the little conference room.

DAMON SHOOK HIS HEAD, unable to believe the state she was in. Shelly Green—easily the most confident woman he'd ever met—looking pale, her eyes wide and panicky. Terrified, even. He reached for her hand, surprised to find it trembling.

"I bet an Ivy Leaguer like you would never freak out like this, would you?" she asked, her voice shaking. "You know, suffer last-minute nerves."

"Is that what this?" he asked, giving her hand a squeeze. "A sudden lack of confidence?"

"I guess beneath the bluster, I'm really just a coward. Who'd have thought, right?" She laughed uneasily.

If anyone was a coward, he was, Damon realized. For trying to brush off his feelings for Shelly; for lacking the confidence to tell his family about her. *They should be here, right now, meeting this amazing woman, watching her make history.*

"You're no coward, Shelly," he said forcefully. "You are one of the most courageous people I've ever known. Just look at what you've managed to accomplish." He waved a hand toward her uniform. "You, all on your own, despite the obstacles, the struggles, the lack of support. You knew what you wanted out of life, and you went for it.

"It doesn't matter where you start," he continued, "or what your family's like or what kind of education you get along the way. It's what kind of person you end up that matters, and look at you." He couldn't help but smile, watching her stare up at him, wide-eyed. "You're about to get your first start in a Sprint Cup race. You accomplished that, Shelly. On your own."

"You're right," she murmured. "I did, didn't I?"

He nodded. "You sure as hell did. With honesty, integrity and perseverance. And you're going to get out there today and show them just how good you are, how ready you are for this. Don't make me drag you out there by your ponytail."

"I can do this," she said, her big blue eyes shining

now as their gazes met and held. She took a deep breath, exhaling slowly as she straightened her spine.

He reached up to cup her face, stroking her cheeks with the pads of his thumbs. "You okay now?"

She nodded. "I'm okay. You know, you should consider going into motivational speaking or something. That was some rousing little pep talk you just gave."

"Yeah, and I meant every word of it." He leaned closer, dipping his head beneath her cap's visor, kissing her softly on the lips before drawing away.

"Thank you," she said, her voice almost a whisper.

"You're welcome. Now I think you better get out there." He tipped his head toward the door. "They're probably out trying to scrounge up another driver by now."

That spurred her into action. "Over my dead body," she said, shaking her head.

"That's the Shelly Green I know," he said with a laugh, leading her back outside. "Awful full of herself for such a little thing."

"Haven't you ever heard that big things come in small packages? Or did I mess up that saying?"

"No, I think you got it just about right. Here's your driver," he called out once they stepped back down to the concrete below. "And she's ready to go."

"Let's go racing, boys!" Shelly said, straightening the brim of her cap with a smile.

The look of relief on Ethan Hunt's face said it all.

SHELLY SAT INSIDE THE cockpit of the car, adjusting her restraints and helmet, ready to get the show on the road.

She glanced out the window, surprised to see Damon still standing at Ethan's side, the pair of them chatting like old buddies.

She felt centered now, completely at ease, and she owed it all to Damon. No one had ever spoken to her with such respect, such admiration. He believed in her, and the truth was, she'd never felt such strong feelings for anyone in all her life.

She loved him.

Didn't matter that she'd only known him a couple of months. It was long enough to know what kind of man he was, enough to know how he made her feel inside.

All warm and tingly.

Smiling to herself, she pulled on her driving gloves and flipped down her visor, ready for the race's call.

It came a minute later. "Lady and gentlemen," a voice boomed out over the loudspeaker. "Start… your…engines."

Immediately, forty-three engines roared to life. Adrenaline began to pump through Shelly's veins, sharpening her focus, pushing out every thought except the race car beneath her, the wheel in her hands.

She'd qualified in the sixteenth spot, so she was starting on row eight, up near the front of the pack. If she could just stay up there, stay out of trouble, and stay out of the wall for 325 laps, it'd be a good day.

Her car was fast, but the track was challenging. Hard on engines because of the sustained RPMs, and hard on tires, too. The pits were tight, which meant she had to be careful on entry and exit.

"Hey, there, chickadee," came a familiar voice over her headset. "I hear you're going for a drive today."

"Al!" Shelly cried, surprised to hear his voice. "What are you doing?"

"Aw, just giving you some moral support. Not that you need it. You're in good hands with Ethan, and don't worry, I told him to make sure he makes you good and mad now and then. Always makes you drive better."

"Yeah, thanks, Al," she said, her voice dripping with sarcasm. She followed the car ahead of her off pit road and onto the track, jerking the wheel back and forth to warm up the tires.

"Anyway, I'll give you back to Ethan, but I ain't moving off this war wagon till you take the checkered flag. Oh, and Shelly? One last thing. You know the… ahem, the suit?"

"Yeah, what about…it?" *Him.* She wanted to say *him,* but knew that this conversation was being listened to by thousands of race fans. Still, she understood his code perfectly—he was talking about Damon.

"A bundle of nerves," Al said. "Try and stay out of the wall, why don't you?"

"Yeah, I was planning to. But thanks for the reminder."

"You got it, chickadee. Now, have some fun out there."

Shelly couldn't help but smile. She *was* going to have fun today, no doubt about it. "Ten-four, Al."

The first caution came twenty-three laps in. A rookie slid up the track in Turn Two and hit the wall, taking out two cars behind him.

"Pits are still closed," came Ethan's voice.

"Got it," Shelly said, relaxing her grip on the wheel.

"How's the car?" Ethan asked.

"Not bad. I'm a little loose in Turns One and Two, but pretty tight in Three and Four. About what we expected."

"Yeah, not much we can do about that. Just part of Atlanta's charm. We'll take two tires. Do you need anything else?"

"I wouldn't mind loosening it up just a little. Can we try a quarter round of wedge?"

"Sure can. Okay, pit road is open this time by."

"Gotcha." Shelly followed the line of cars down onto pit road, carefully watching her tachometer. Last thing she needed was a speeding penalty.

"Okay," came Ethan's voice. "Four, three, two, one."

Shelly stopped on a dime, perfectly positioned in her pit stall. She let out a sigh of relief as her over-the-wall crew serviced the car. Fourteen-point-seven seconds later, she pulled out just ahead of the car she'd pitted behind.

Not bad, not bad at all.

"Great stop, boys," she said as she pulled back out onto the track.

"You're in the eighth spot now, Shelly," Ethan said. "Just see if you can hold that track position. There's still a lot of racing left."

"Ten-four, Ethan."

"One more to go before we go green."

"I'm ready." Shelly flipped up her visor to wipe the perspiration from her eyes, then flipped it back down again. Damn, it was hot inside that car, and likely to get hotter before the day was out.

As soon as the green flag waved, Shelly laid on the throttle. Other than her spotter's voice, her radio remained silent as she rocketed around the track on the high groove, hitting her marks with practiced precision. There were definite benefits to running the NASCAR Nationwide Series race the day before, she realized. She was comfortable with the track today, even more so than she had been the day before.

Trouble came on lap fifty-six as Shelly went too high in turn two and tapped the wall—a light tap, but enough to cause concern. The last thing she needed was damage to her car this early on.

"Sorry about that," Shelly said into her mike, silently cursing herself. "I just lost it. Didn't have any grip there."

"I think we're okay," Ethan said. "Will Branch is in the lead, and he's probably going to pit in a few laps. Just follow him in, and we'll check out that right-side quarter panel to make sure we don't have any tire rub."

Shelly gripped the wheel, trying to assess the damage. A little vibration, but nothing out of the ordinary. "Right now it feels okay."

"Looks okay, too. Just try and hold off Justin Murphy, if you can. Are you getting any looser?"

"Nah, just losing grip. The track is eating up my tires."

"Okay, shouldn't be more than a lap or two till the pit cycle starts. Just hang in there."

"Will do," Shelly said. One mistake—one little mistake—but she wasn't going to let it shake her confidence. She'd only lost two spots, and the handling hadn't gotten any worse. If this was the worst mistake she made all day, then she couldn't complain too much.

All she had to do was hang on for two-hundred-and-sixty-something more laps, and she'd get a top-ten finish. Yeah, piece of cake. Like always, she was racing to win, but heck, she'd take a top-ten in her first NASCAR Sprint Cup Series start.

After what felt like forever but was probably only a couple of minutes later, the leader pulled onto pit road, and Shelly followed suit. The pit crew took a little longer than usual, taking some time to bang out the dented quarter panel, but she only lost two positions. She could live with that. After all, it was better to lose the track position than to risk blowing a tire.

FIFTY LAPS TO GO. Damon knew the fuel window was fifty to fifty-five laps at this particular track, so that meant these pit stops were likely the last before the checkered flag, unless there was a caution.

He let out his breath in a rush when the Greenstone Garden Centers car raced off pit road, gaining another spot and moving into fourth position as it rocketed into Turn One, a blur of blue and yellow. As always, he could barely believe that Shelly was behind the wheel of that car. *Unbelievable.*

Watching her out there, it was obvious that she'd fully recovered from her earlier confidence issues. He shook his head in utter amazement as she dropped low and took the third spot from Will Branch, an experienced NASCAR Sprint Cup Series driver.

In fact, all the drivers up front with her were experienced drivers. Yet she was holding her own with them, as if she'd been racing them all season. She might be new to this series, but she could clearly compete with the best of them, with the most seasoned drivers—with former champions, for that matter.

Just like Pebble Valley Winery. The thought came from seemingly nowhere, and yet he immediately recognized it as the truth. She was just like their winery. Didn't matter where she finished today—she'd already proven herself worthy of driving in this series.

After today, everyone would be talking about Shelly Green. They would respect her, admire her talent. And what's more, if she spoke highly of Pebble Valley Wines, they'd trust her. People would go out and buy Pebble Valley Wines, simply because Shelly Green was associated with them. And wasn't that what a sponsorship was all about?

He swallowed hard, realizing what that meant. The sponsorship…it should be hers. And not because he found her attractive, not because she made him laugh, not because he couldn't be around her without wanting to kiss her senseless, but because she deserved it.

And there was more, he realized. He loved her. It didn't matter that they came from different backgrounds, different worlds. Didn't matter that he knew investments and she knew cars, that he loved escargot and she wouldn't touch them with a ten-foot pole. What's more, he didn't give a rat's ass what his family would think. He didn't want their approval, didn't need it.

He'd spent four years dating Courtney, and he'd never been exactly sure how he felt about her. Yet he'd barely known Shelly two months, and he was one-hundred-percent sure he wanted to spend the rest of his life with her, marveling at her.

If only she would let him.

He watched her race into Turn Four, still in third position with less than ten laps to go, and realized that he had no idea how deeply her affections for him ran. She'd admitted to having feelings for him, yes. But was she as crazy about him as he was about her? As willing to throw caution to the wind, to overlook their differences? He had to know, had to find out before he drove himself crazy. Tonight.

But first things first. She had a race to finish, and a sponsorship to accept.

CHAPTER SIXTEEN

"SHELLY, THREE TO GO at the line. Just keep doing what you're doing," Ethan said.

"How are we on fuel? Are we going to make it?" A caution five laps back had left them with a tough decision—stay out and keep their track position, or duck onto pit road for a splash of fuel. Ethan had suggested the former, and Shelly had agreed.

Might as well go for it. All the lead cars were taking the same gamble she was, hoping to stretch their fuel mileage. At this point, all she could do was hope for the best and try to preserve her position.

Garrett Clark was out in front now, Justin Murphy right behind him. They were far enough ahead that she couldn't catch them, not while attempting to save fuel. Will Branch had taken the third spot back from Shelly just before the last caution. She might be able to catch him, but she didn't have much time left. On the other hand, trying might waste fuel. It might end up costing her a top-five finish.

Just ride it out, she told herself, trying to ignore the ache that had begun at her shoulders and now reached all the way to her wrists. Still, she kept her gaze locked on the gold-and-black bumper of Branch's No. 467 car, just hoping for an opportunity to get around him without much struggle.

"White flag next time by, Shelly," Ethan said, his voice tense.

Which told her that he was worried. He wasn't sure she could make it. *Damn.* So much for trying to catch Branch. It was just too risky. As much as she wanted to advance her position, she wanted to finish more.

The flagstand went by in a blur, white flag waving. Four more turns, that was all. In Turn One, she headed for the high line—the best line for old tires—and stayed high in Turn Two, dropping back to the middle in the back straightaway. The nose of her car edged up toward Branch's bumper, getting him a little loose.

He accelerated as they headed into Turn Three, increasing the distance between them. Shelly gritted her teeth, resting her right arm on the wheel slightly as they headed into the last turn.

"Branch is out of gas!" came Ethan's voice in her headset.

A bubble of excitement welled in Shelly's chest as she saw him duck low, coasting now. She zipped by, headed straight for the finish line. A celebration erupted in her headset as she took the checkered flag, the voices indistinguishable as they whooped it up.

"Great race, Shelly," Ethan said, discernable at last. "A third-place finish in your first-ever start in the series! What do you say to that?"

"Woo-hoo!" she yelled, tears welling in her eyes. "Thanks, guys. You were awesome today!"

Minutes later, she rolled onto pit road and cut the engine. Her arms trembling from fatigue, she removed her helmet and HANS device, then dropped the net and climbed out of the car while Garrett Clark made his victory doughnuts, the crowd roaring in appreciation.

Seconds later, her team surrounded her in celebration—her surrogate team, Trey's team, lifting her off her feet time and again in big bear hugs. Once they set her back on her feet, someone handed her a blue Greenstone Garden Centers cap and a cold bottle of water, which she downed almost entirely in one long gulp.

As soon as she wiped her sweaty brow and pulled her ponytail through the back of the cap, she saw Damon headed her way, flashing her his movie-star smile—as if her knees weren't already weak enough after five hundred miles of racing in eighty-something degree heat.

"Hey, Shelly," he called out, and Shelly noticed that he held his cell phone open in one hand. "So, how would you like to be the face of Pebble Valley Winery?"

"What did you say?" she asked, momentarily stunned. Did he mean…was he offering her the sponsorship?

"I'm saying that the Pebble Valley sponsorship is yours. If you want it, that is." He raked one hand through his hair, as was his habit when he was nervous, she realized.

"Just like that?" she sputtered. Her heart went from a slow canter to a full-out gallop. "I didn't think…I mean, I thought…" Damn, but she couldn't even form a coherent sentence, and the pit road reporters would be descending on her any minute now. She could see them up ahead, interviewing Justin Murphy.

"Here." Damon thrust his cell phone into her hand. "It's Steve Clayton."

She put the phone to her ear, covering her other one so she could hear above the din of the crowd. "Hello?" she yelled.

"Hey, it's the new face of Pebble Valley!" Steve yelled back. "Or haven't you accepted yet?"

"Thank *you*, Steve," she managed to choke out before she threw her arms around Damon's neck, almost dropping the phone in the process.

"And thank *you*," she said against his neck, breathing in his clean, masculine scent. "I don't know what made you change your mind, but thank you."

Be professional, she reminded herself, releasing him and taking a step back, her cheeks burning.

He took the phone from her and held it to his ear. "She accepts. I'll call you later." With that, he snapped it shut and shoved it back into his pocket.

"Congratulations," he said, his voice so soft, so full of emotion that it made her heart stutter. Somehow that word meant so much more when he said it, though she couldn't say why.

And then Adam Sanford came pushing through the crowd, wrapping her in a hug.

"Hey, boss man," Shelly said. "That was some ride."

"Sure was. I knew you could do it." He released her and stepped back, smiling like the cat who had swallowed the proverbial canary. "I suppose Tieri told you the news?"

"He sure did."

Adam nodded. "It's not a done deal, not yet, but I'd say you're on your way to a permanent ride."

"I still can't believe it," Shelly murmured, still feeling slightly dazed.

"You better believe it," Damon said.

"Wow," she managed to say. "Just…wow. I feel like Cinderella."

"Anyway," Adam said, patting her on the shoulder, "we'll talk more on the plane ride home. Here come the reporters." He tipped his head toward the camera equipment that was headed their way. "I'll let you have your moment in the limelight."

"Thanks, Adam," she murmured.

"Anytime." With a salute, he disappeared.

"Can we celebrate tonight?" Damon asked, watching the reporters' approach over the top of her head. "When we get back to Mooresville? Or is that too much excitement for one day?"

"No, I'd like that," Shelly said. "It's a short flight home. We can have a late dinner or something."

"Sounds good. Call me when you land, and I'll pick you up. Don't worry about dressing up or anything. We'll just get takeout or something at my place."

"It's a date," Shelly said, then wished she could take it back. He probably didn't intend for it to be a date—more of a business celebration thing. A sponsor-driver get-together. Great, now he was going to think that she'd misinterpreted his invitation. How embarrassing.

It occurred to her that, as the face of Pebble Valley

Winery, she'd probably be working pretty closely with him in the coming year. Which, now that she thought about it, was going to be tricky considering the fact that she'd gone and fallen in love with him.

Uh-oh. Smart move, Shelly.

She was saved thinking about it further by the droves of reporters that suddenly surrounded her, all jockeying for position.

With a wink, Damon disappeared into the crowd.

SHELLY GLANCED AT HER reflection in her compact mirror one last time as the plane touched down on the tarmac in North Carolina. After she'd given her requisite post-race interviews, she'd taken a quick shower in her motor home, and then tried on everything she'd brought with her to Atlanta, trying to find something casual yet feminine to wear.

Finally, she'd settled on a pair of khaki capris and a long, tunic-style top that skimmed her hips. The top was a little too colorful, too bohemian for her tastes, but it would have to do.

She'd left her hair down, her bangs released from the clip she now used to keep them out of her eyes. Luckily, she'd brought along the makeup she'd bought with Becky, so she'd managed to brush on a little eyeshadow and mascara during the quick flight home. She just needed to add some lip gloss and she was ready.

As the plane taxied to a stop, she took out her cell phone and scrolled through her contacts till she found Damon's number. Her fingers shook as she punched the button to connect the call, but as soon as she heard his voice, her nerves seemed to vanish at once.

"Hi, there. I see your plane," he said. "I'll meet you when you get off."

"Okay," she murmured with a smile. It felt like forever since she'd seen him last. How long had it actually been? No more than a couple of hours.

Five minutes later she stepped down onto the tarmac, her eyes widening with surprise.

Damon stood there carrying a small bouquet of flowers, a purple satin ribbon wrapped around their stems. The blooms were all hues of blues, from pale blue to cornflower blue to deep indigo.

"They reminded me of your eyes," he said, offering her the bouquet. "Congratulations again."

"Thanks," she said, taking the flowers with tears dampening her lashes. No one had ever given her flowers before—never, in all her life. She bent over the bouquet, inhaling the fragrance. "Wow, you really shouldn't have."

He probably bought women flowers all the time, she realized. It just illustrated how different their lives were. The men she'd dated in the past had given her things like oil pumps and ignition switches. Not that she'd complained. In fact, she'd appreciated the gifts. And not that she was dating Damon.

This was…a business meeting. Nothing more, nothing less.

"I ordered some Italian food," he said, leading her toward his car. A station wagon, albeit a fancy German import, with New York plates. "Hope that's okay."

"Sounds good." She was starving, actually. A plate of pasta would definitely hit the spot.

He opened the door for her, and she climbed in. "Nice ride," she teased, once he climbed into the driver's seat and started the ignition. "Very safe and reliable."

"Please don't make fun of my car. You'll hurt her feelings."

"Her?"

"You know, like a ship. Aren't ships always female?"

Shelly shook her head, laughing. "I have no clue. Are they?"

Damon nodded. "I think so."

"So, does she have a name?"

A smile played at the corner of his lips. "Of course. Her name is Greta. You know, like Garbo."

"Huh." *I'm in love with a banker guy who names his car.* "Anything else I should know about you before we embark on this business relationship, Mr. Tieri? Don't tell me you have a cat. Or worse, cats. Plural. Trixie would never approve."

"Speaking of the little mutt, where is she?"

"She rode home in the motor home with Charlie. To keep him company."

"And to answer your question, no," Damon said.

"No what?" Shelly asked. She'd forgotten the question.

"No, I'm not some crazy cat guy. Not that I dislike cats, I like them just fine. But I worked such long, irregular hours at TCM that I never really had time for a pet."

"That's sad, Tieri. Okay, anything else? You know, since we'll be business associates and all."

She saw him take a deep breath.

"I have a soft spot for women with freckles," he said. "And ponytails, apparently."

Shelly's breath hitched in her chest, but she vowed to play it cool. "Oh, yeah? Interesting. What else?"

"Blond hair. Blue eyes. About yea high." Keeping his eyes on the road, he held out one hand at shoulder height. "Driving race cars is a bonus."

Shelly decided to play along. "Interestingly enough, I know someone who fits that description."

"Yeah? But how does she feel about Wall Street types? You know, those fuddy-duddy money managers who don't contribute much to the greater good of society?"

"Oh, shut up," Shelly said with a smile.

"You said it, not me." He turned off the main road, headed toward his rental on Lake Norman.

"I say a lot of things. You should learn to take half of them with a grain of salt."

"I'll remember that."

"Anyway, to answer *your* question," Shelly ventured, gathering her courage, "she finds them sexy. Very, very sexy."

It was his turn to look surprised. "Really?"

"Hey, keep your eyes on the road. Are we *ever* going to get to your house?" Shelly asked impatiently, her skin flushed.

"It's this one, right here." He turned down a long, curving drive. Up ahead, floodlights lit a multi-storied, rambling Mediterranean.

"Wow," Shelly muttered. "When you said *rental* I just assumed…well, I didn't picture *this*."

"Yeah, it's nice, isn't it? The owner decided to put it on the market. I was thinking of selling my co-op in New York and buying it. Might even get myself a boat."

Shelly just shook her head. "You're really embracing the lifestyle, aren't you? NASCAR, I mean."

Pulling around a fountain in the middle of the circular drive, he cut the motor and turned to face her. "This *is* my life now. And I want you to be a part of it. Permanently."

"You mean…a business relationship?"

He shook his head. "No, not just that. I want more. I want *you*."

For a moment, Shelly couldn't speak. She simply stared at him, wondering if she was imagining things. This whole day…everything about it had been surreal. The race, the sponsorship, and now *this*. It seemed too perfect, everything tied up in a neat little bow. Real life didn't work that way—or did it?

Apparently Damon misinterpreted her silence. "I'm sorry," he said. "I shouldn't have said that. I know it's too soon. It's just that I've never felt so sure—"

"Shut up and kiss me, Damon," Shelly interrupted. "Now."

CHAPTER SEVENTEEN

IT TOOK THEM A FULL ten minutes to get from the car to the front door. One kiss led to another, each more heated, more passionate than the one before it. Once they stepped inside, their hands were seemingly everywhere at once. Various pieces of clothing were shed along the way, leaving a trail from the front door up the stairs to the master bedroom.

Damon paused only long enough to sweep her into his arms, carrying her into his room, kicking the door shut behind him before laying her down on his bed.

An hour later, Shelly curled against his chest, cradled in his arms. The moon had risen high in the sky, framed in the window beside the bed, casting silvery light across her smooth, perfect skin.

"Wow," she said, her breath still coming fast. "Just… wow."

"You can say that again." He stroked her hair, as soft as silk. For perhaps another ten minutes, they lay in perfect silence.

Damon had never felt so happy, so satisfied, so sated in all his life. He should have known that making love to Shelly would be as life-changing as everything else about her was. She had that kind of effect on people; she couldn't help it.

"The food's probably cold by now," he murmured against her hair.

"Food? Who needs food?" she said sleepily.

"You do," he said, disentangling himself from her limbs and reaching for a pair of jeans. "I promised you dinner, remember?"

She sat up, clutching a sheet around her as she rubbed her eyes. "Maybe. I guess I *am* kind of hungry."

"Don't go anywhere," he said, pausing at the door. "I'll be back in five minutes."

When he returned, carrying a steaming platter of spaghetti with meat sauce, she was standing by the window, gazing out at the lake, wearing one of his button-down shirts. The French cuffs hung down past her wrists, the shirttails almost reached her knees.

"You look perfect," he said, unable to hide the awe in his voice. "So incredibly beautiful." With her pale, tousled hair falling around her shoulders, her long legs stretching out from the hem of his shirt, she looked as sexy as hell. And she was entirely his, he mentally added.

She turned to face him with a heart-stopping smile, pushing her hair back from her eyes. "Mmm, spaghetti. Okay, now I'm starved."

He set the tray down on the bedside table. "Before you can eat, you have to answer one question. Well, first you have to hear me out. Then answer one question. Deal?"

"You're quite the negotiator, aren't you? Okay,

shoot." She leaned back against the window, the small of her back pressed to the sill as she stretched languorously. The hem of the shirt rose dangerously high, the view making his pulse leap.

He took a deep breath before he spoke, knowing he needed to get this right. "I'm in love with you, Shelly. I think I have been since that night in Daytona, since Adam Sanford left us alone at that table. I know it seems fast—some would say rash, even. But I know how I feel, and for once in my life, I'm following my heart. Charting my own course.

"I want to marry you, if you'll have me. That's where the question comes in," he said, pausing to watch her expression, to watch her blue eyes widen. "*Will* you have me, Shelly?"

"You're asking me to marry you?"

"I probably did it badly," he said, running a hand through his hair. "I'm sorry about that. I wish I had a ring. I probably should have gotten down on one knee."

He could have sworn he saw tears in her eyes as she shook her head. "You did it perfectly, Damon. And to answer your question, yes. Yes!" She launched herself into his arms, wrapping her legs around his waist, her arms around his neck.

"Forget the spaghetti," he said, just as her mouth found his and they fell back to the bed in a tangled heap.

January

SHELLY LAUGHED AS SHE allowed her husband to help her out of the car, blindfolded. *Her husband.* She still marveled every time she thought the words. Seven months ago, Damon Tieri had been a total stranger to her. And now he was her husband.

Her gorgeous, proud, sometimes maddening husband. He was also the sweetest, most generous man she'd ever met.

The wedding had been simple, yet beautiful—the ceremony in a little stone church on Martha's Vineyard, where they'd flown in their guests, just family and a few close friends. Damon's parents, obviously baffled by their youngest son's engagement and by the speed at which the events leading up to the wedding progressed, were surprisingly accommodating, hosting a dinner reception at their beach house on the bluff in Aquinnah—which, as it turned out, was much bigger than the "little cottage" Damon had described. Missy, still sober and looking great in her pale-blue dinner suit, had managed to keep herself in check, doing nothing more embarrassing than sobbing loudly during the ceremony. All in all, it had been perfect.

Somehow, Becky had managed to help her find the perfect wedding dress—a strapless silk shantung number with a pale-blue sash—and then made sure it was altered to fit in record time. In fact, she and Becky had grown so close that Shelly had asked her to serve as her only attendant. Becky had worn a deep-blue gown, looking as gorgeous as ever. Damon's brother Mario had served as best man, and the pair of them—the Tieri brothers—had looked stunningly handsome in their white dinner jackets and tuxedo pants.

Inside the chapel, there had been candles everywhere, and they were surrounded by flowers in every hue of blue. A string quartet had provided the music, and when Al Spencer had walked her down the aisle to the traditional wedding march with tears in his eyes, Shelly had felt like a princess—like Cinderella, with her Prince Charming waiting for her there at the altar.

Without a doubt, it had been the happiest day of her life. Even winning her first-ever NASCAR Nationwide Series championship just weeks before the wedding had paled in comparison, as had the day that Adam Sanford called to tell her that he was going to field a second NASCAR Sprint Cup Series car next season, and the ride was hers if she wanted it. As it happened, there had been more than one offer from established NASCAR Sprint Cup teams for her to choose from. Didn't matter, though. Adam Sanford had launched her career—she wasn't abandoning him now. He was like family.

So come next month, she'd be driving the Pebble Valley Winery car full-time in the NASCAR Sprint Cup Series, and the ZippiPrint car part-time in the NASCAR Nationwide Series. It was going to be a busy year, that much was certain. She could barely wait.

She sighed loudly, brought back to the present as she allowed Damon to lead her twenty yards from the car, stumbling blindly all the way. "You can't keep me blindfolded forever, you know," she said, tightly gripping Damon's arm. "It would definitely be a workplace liability."

In the distance, she could hear the crash of waves.

Taking a deep breath, she inhaled salt-scented air that could only mean they were near the ocean.

"Okay, what is this? We already had a honeymoon." In Hawaii. Two idyllic weeks of sun and surf, with hot, sticky nights that she wished could have lasted forever.

"Keep your eyes closed," Damon said, his hands working the knot of fabric at the back of her head. "I'm taking off the blindfold now, but don't open your eyes till I tell you to look."

"Okay, okay. I get it."

"And no peeking."

Shelly *harrumphed,* though of course she had meant to peek through her lashes. Truth was, she didn't like surprises. Half the time they fell flat, and she wanted time to prepare her expression, just in case.

"Are you going to stomp your foot, too?" Damon asked with a laugh.

He was enjoying this, she could tell. *Way* too much.

Finally the fabric folds fell away, the chilled breeze hitting her face with full force. She must have shivered.

"Are you cold?"

Shelly shook her head, her eyes still squeezed shut. "Nah, I'm fine."

"Good. Okay, you can open your eyes now," Damon said, his voice soft.

She did, and stood blinking in the bright winter sunshine for what felt like an eternity. Directly in front of her loomed an enormous beachfront lot surrounded by jetties and dunes. Behind the lot, over a jetty and across a perfect crescent beach, enormous, foam-tipped waves crashed. Off toward the horizon, the sun was dipping down toward the water, turning the sky a brilliant pink.

"It's beautiful," she said at last, releasing the breath she hadn't realized she'd been holding. "But...I don't get it. It's kind of cold for the beach this time of year, isn't it? Here, at least." Unlike Hawaii...

He smiled, the corners of his dark eyes crinkling with the effort. "We're not on vacation." Reaching into his pocket, he removed a folded brochure listing a well-known architect. "It's yours," he said, handing her the brochure. "The land, for your beach house. We're meeting with the architect in an hour."

Shelly's mind stumbled, trying to grasp the situation. "Mine?"

"Yeah, yours," he said with a shrug.

"You bought me land for a beach house?" she asked incredulously.

He turned to glance back at the lot, and then back at her again. "Remember that night on the beach in Daytona? You said you'd always dreamed of owning a beach house. In the Outer Banks. So I thought it might be a nice wedding present. You know, from me to you. Just tell the architect exactly what you want."

Unable to speak a single word, Shelly just continued to stand there gaping like an idiot. *My dream house, on the ocean.*

Tears filled her eyes, began spilling down her cheeks unchecked. All these years, she'd had no one to rely on, not even her mother, no one to make her wishes come true but herself. And now Damon… She shook her head, letting the thought trail off as she stared at the magnificent piece of property. It felt good to let someone take care of her for a change, to have an ally, someone who remembered little things that she'd said, someone who wanted to make all her dreams come true. She reached up to wipe away her tears, still too choked up to speak.

Obviously misinterpreting her reaction, Damon swore under his breath. "I knew I should have asked you first. Of course you'd want to be part of the decision, want to pick out the land yourself. We can put it on the market tomorrow. It shouldn't be too hard to get rid of."

She shook her head, trying to find the right words. "No, Damon. I'm just…speechless, that's all. It's the nicest thing anyone has ever done for me." She was choking on the words now. "I love it," she said, throwing her arms around his neck. "It's absolutely perfect, Damon. Just like you."

She kissed him on the lips, intending it to be a quick, chaste kiss. Instead, she found herself opening her mouth against his, kissing him so deeply, so hungrily that she felt it all the way to her toes.

"I guess that means you like it?" he asked when she finally pulled away, breathless.

She nodded, reaching for the brochure. "I like it. C'mon, let's go check it out. I'm dying to see the view from that dune." She pointed to the highest point on the property, a gently sloping tan-colored dune off toward the right.

"How about if we go check out the secluded little cove instead, Mrs. Tieri?" he asked, grinning wickedly.

Shelly rolled her eyes as she dragged Damon toward the sand dunes. "I told you, I'm *not* changing my name. It was a deal-breaker. You agreed, remember?"

He shrugged, his eyes gleaming playfully. "I can't help it if I'm traditional. You know, it's that fuddy-duddy banker in me. Anyway, can't I at least call you Mrs. Tieri in private? Here at our beach house, at least?"

"Maybe," she agreed. "But only at our beach house."

"Deal," he said, sweeping her off her feet and carrying over what would become the threshold of their new home—toward their future. "You drive a hard bargain. Mrs. Tieri," he added, kissing her lightly on the nose.

"Oh, man, you're going to drive me nuts with that now, aren't you? I never should have agreed."

"Well, it's only fair. I have to share Shelly Green with her adoring fans from, what? February through November? At least give me December and January to have Shelly Tieri all to myself."

"Okay, okay. Sheesh." She was teasing him, of course. As always. "You can put me down any time you want, you know."

"I know," he agreed, though he held her more closely to his chest. "I'll race you to the cove."

"Keep in mind, I'm fast. *Very* fast."

"Yeah, a force of nature," he agreed. "That's exactly what you are."

"What does that even mean?" she asked, pressing her cheek against his heart, listening to it thump against his ribs. She could stay like this forever, safe and secure, in his arms.

"Just that I'm one lucky man." Gently, he set her on her feet, pressing a kiss to her neck, just below her ear.

"Mmm, start your engines," she murmured, laughing as she led him toward the crashing waves.

Damon glanced down at his watch. "Like I said, we're meeting with the architect in an hour. Let's get to that cove—no time to waste."

Shelly nodded. It was going to be one heck of an hour, she realized. One heck of a life, she corrected.

Starting *now*.

* * * * *

*For more thrill-a-minute romances set against the
exciting backdrop of the NASCAR world, don't miss:
BANKING ON HOPE by Maggie Price
Available in December
For a sneak peek, just turn the page!*

"How's your work for my brother going?" he asked.

"Slow and methodical, which is the norm for the beginning of a project. I've met individually with all of the employees. That's the first step when I do team building."

"How'd that go? Interacting with guys who know you've been hired to probe their minds."

She sent him a pointed look. "Adam agreed to my request to explain to his people the first day why he hired me. I didn't want any of them to think I was there to play ping-pong with their brains."

"Draw any conclusions, yet?"

"When I do, I'll discuss them with Adam."

Brent held up a hand. "He's your client, not me—I understand that. I just figure you'll be spending the next few days watching the team practice. Then observing them at the race on Saturday."

"That's right."

"If you want any pointers on race day, just ask."

Something flashed in her gray eyes. "You'll be there? At the track?"

"That's the plan." He lifted a brow. "Surprised?"

"Totally. Adam mentioned that you pretty much avoid anything NASCAR."

"He's right."

"So, why come to the race track this weekend?"

Because you'll be there. "Trey's still off the schedule. Adam needs an experienced, unbiased driver to evaluate Shelly Green's performance this weekend."

"Since he's letting her drive Trey's car, I would think Adam has a lot of faith in her."

"He does. But this isn't just about one race. He's considering offering her a NASCAR Sprint Cup ride next season. That's not something a team owner does lightly."

"Of course not." Hope's brow furrowed. "Have you been to many NASCAR races since…"

"Talladega," Brent finished when her voice trailed off. "Saturday will be the first time in four years that I've stepped foot on a NASCAR-sanctioned track. As you might imagine, I don't get the warmest welcome from most people in the business." It was his turn to give her the pointed look. "The majority of them think I'm a cheater who tried to sabotage a competitor's car."

Watching her gaze slide from his as she set down her coffee, told him she belonged in that category. "Some people don't share that opinion," she said.

"Really? Who?"

"The reception at the terminal in Charlotte. She told me about how you went out of your way to find her son a rare NASCAR miniature race car for his birthday."

"That wasn't a big deal."

"To her it was. She basically thinks you walk on water."

"Yeah?" Brent leaned in. "What do you think, doc?"

"That someone who makes that kind of effort for a child must have some redeeming qualities."

"So you think I maybe have some good points?"

"Everyone has good points. Sometimes they're just hard to find."

"Want to try to find mine?"

She opened her mouth. He would never know what she had been about to say because at that moment, her name blared on the PA system.

"My ride's here," she said, rising.

Brent stood, held out his hand. "See you at the track for the race, doc."

She hesitated before she slid her palm against his. Her skin felt soft and warm, much the same as it had in his dream.

"See you," she replied. Then she grabbed the handle of her small suitcase and disappeared around a corner.

Too bad he couldn't get her out of his head that easily.

Abby Gaines
THE COMEBACK

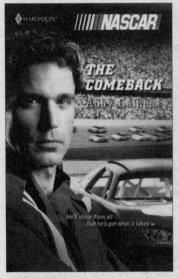

Making a comeback to
drive his family's team to
victory in the NASCAR
Sprint Cup Series,
Zack Matheson doesn't
want any distractions—
and that includes
Gaby Colson, the sexy
PR rep hired to promote
his single-guy image. But
as heat sizzles between
them, Gaby is determined
to show Zack that his
comeback won't be
complete without her.

*Available February 2010
wherever books are sold.*

www.GetYourHeartRacing.com

REQUEST YOUR FREE BOOKS!

2 FREE NOVELS
FROM THE ROMANCE/SUSPENSE
COLLECTION PLUS 2 FREE GIFTS!

YES! Please send me 2 FREE novels from the Romance/Suspense Collection and my 2 FREE gifts (gifts are worth about $10). After receiving them, if I don't wish to receive any more books, I can return the shipping statement marked "cancel." If I don't cancel, I will receive 4 brand-new novels every month and be billed just $5.74 per book in the U.S. or $6.24 per book in Canada. That's a savings of at least 28% off the cover price. It's quite a bargain! Shipping and handling is just 50¢ per book.* I understand that accepting the 2 free books and gifts places me under no obligation to buy anything. I can always return a shipment and cancel at any time. Even if I never buy another book from the Reader Service, the two free books and gifts are mine to keep forever.   185 MDN EYNQ   385 MDN EYN2

Name	(PLEASE PRINT)

Address	Apt. #

City	State/Prov.	Zip/Postal Code

Signature (if under 18, a parent or guardian must sign)

Mail to **The Reader Service:**
IN U.S.A.: P.O. Box 1867, Buffalo, NY 14240-1867
IN CANADA: P.O. Box 609, Fort Erie, Ontario L2A 5X3

Not valid to current subscribers of the Romance Collection,
the Suspense Collection or the Romance/Suspense Collection.

Want to try two free books from another line?
Call 1-800-873-8635 or visit www.morefreebooks.com.

* Terms and prices subject to change without notice. Prices do not include applicable taxes. Sales tax applicable in N.Y. Canadian residents will be charged applicable provincial taxes and GST. Offer not valid in Quebec. This offer is limited to one order per household. All orders subject to approval. Credit or debit balances in a customer's account(s) may be offset by any other outstanding balance owed by or to the customer. Please allow 4 to 6 weeks for delivery. Offer available while quantities last.

BOB09

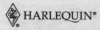